South USA

A Sense of Home

To Will,
Thanks for your support !

Jerry Smith

Jerry Smith

outskirts
press

Disclaimer:

This novel's story and characters are fictitious. The South Amboy setting is also fictitious and in no way depicts the author's hometown of South Amboy, New Jersey, or any of its past or present residents. The role played by Jerome Emiliani is entirely fictional; although the author did draw inspiration from what little is known about the life of Saint Jerome Emiliani, the patron saint of abandoned children.

"There is no greater agony than bearing an untold story inside of you."

-Maya Angelou

PROLOGUE

It's a perfect spring morning in New York City, and I'm sipping my first cup of coffee of the day. Sitting on a bench under a cloudless blue sky in Central Park, I'm surrounded by a flock of pigeons looking for a handout, but I have nothing to offer. The blue-gray birds fascinate me, though, as they strut and fan their tails while making throaty coos until the chiming ringtone of my cell phone interrupts the moment.

The caller is Andrew Leahy, the former leader and principal songwriter for a 1980s-era pop music band known as the Overseas Highwaymen. The Florida Keys-based group was on the brink of superstardom but broke up under curious circumstances. Many in the music industry and the public still wonder why things fell apart for the group.

"Is this Mr. Zach Schultz, the music journalist?" Leahy asks.

In 2005, my then-editor asked me to write an article about one-hit wonders—artists who'd had a Top 40 single but could never repeat that achievement. The Overseas Highwaymen fit that category. However, the magazine never published the proposed article, and Andrew Leahy remained an obscure figure in pop music history.

Leahy assures me the unpublished article is of no consequence. Instead, he begins by complimenting me on my latest book, a decade-by-decade guide to popular music. He refers to my chapter about the 1980s, which mentions the Overseas Highwaymen as a mere sidenote. After a brief pause, he says he has a "story" in which I may be interested and suggests I could develop it into a full-length novel. He wants to talk about it in person.

I've had book ideas pitched to me before, and I've always dismissed them. I'm a music journalist, not a novelist. Yet, despite my general skepticism, I am intrigued and still harbor several questions surrounding the breakup of the Overseas Highwaymen. My curiosity gets the best of me. "What sort of story?"

Leahy refuses to say more. He suggests I meet him in his hometown of South Amboy because that's where most of the events he wants to tell me about took place.

He has me on the hook, and I think he knows it. "Fine," I tell him. "I'll come to you." We meet the following week at the café he now owns and operates in South Amboy. In the interim, I prepare for our meeting by digging out my notes from 2005 and jotting down a few questions for Mr. Leahy. I recall how vague he'd been so long ago and wonder if I'm in for a similar experience. If Leahy plays coy with me again, our meeting will be very brief.

A week later, I arrive at the train station in South Amboy, and Leahy picks me up in his late-model pickup truck. After a few minutes of becoming reacquainted, instead of taking me directly to the café, he gives me a driving tour of the town, pointing out the places where he'd gone to school and church, and played baseball. Finally, he takes me down to the waterfront and parks his truck so we are looking at Ampoge Bay. He tells me Ampoge is a Native American word. He points to the lighthouse not far offshore and reminisces about how he used to *borrow* his father's sailboat without permission to go out there. I get the idea of Leahy conveying his strong connection to this town, but I'm eager to hear about his departure from the Overseas Highwaymen in 1985, and I'm not sure what the sights and sounds of South Amboy have to do with that.

"Can't we just get down to business?" I ask.

He agrees and starts the engine. We continue to drive along the waterfront area and park in the lot of Clare's Music Café, the place he'd mentioned on the phone. By the time we walk into the busy establishment, it is nearly lunchtime. Patrons are waiting for takeout or dining in.

"Are you hungry?" he asks.

"Yes," I admit, having had only a bowl of instant oatmeal before leaving my apartment that morning.

"Great!" He summons a female server to take my order. "We can have your order brought directly to my office in the back."

Leahy takes me to a theater, which he refers to as "the listening room." The facility boasts a state-of-the-art sound system and cushioned seating for about 150 people.

From there, we go to his private office at the rear of the theater. When my lunch arrives, he insists I eat before we get into any real discussion. Meanwhile, he entertains me with idle chitchat about how the theater serves the South Amboy community.

After I've eaten, Leahy smiles and says he has stipulations. He requires me to *fictionalize* the story, and he insists I not use any real names, including his name and the name of his hometown because many people involved are still around. His other stipulation is that I must suspend my disbelief or call on whatever faith I can muster. He claims his story is true, and he insists I trust him to write a believable story.

Stipulations? I inform Leahy he is not about to dictate any terms to me.

To appease me, Leahy dangles a carrot by promising to divulge the real reason he left the Overseas Highwaymen and the Florida Keys in 1985. We go back and forth until I agree to hear his tale. If I decide not to write his story as a work of fiction, I will maintain his confidence. If I write it, Leahy can have the final say about how I fictionalize the story. I figure it's his story. Whatever I choose to believe will be up to me.

Sitting in the back office of Clare's Music Cafe, Andrew Leahy speaks with such clarity and passion that I dare not interrupt. After hearing his experiences, I agree to write a fictionalized version of his story according to his terms—or at least try. The characters and South Amboy setting are products of my imagination. Readers will have to use their discretion regarding the possibilities Mr. Leahy proposes.

1

ANDREW

Dressed in a tropical print shirt, faded beige shorts, and light chino high-top sneakers with no socks, thirty-four-year-old Andrew Leahy looked every bit the irresponsible beach bum his family and friends thought he would be. Coarse facial stubble added to this image. Leahy opened the French door that led to the sundeck of his newly purchased, three-bedroom waterfront home on Lower Sugarloaf Key, Florida. Beyond the narrow sparsely vegetated beach, he could see from his vantage point that the water was rougher than usual in the premature twilight, brought on by a thickening, anvil-shaped layer of clouds. Stepping onto the deck, the tropical evening's sea-scented air caressed his sunburned face as lightning flickered rhythmically in the distance. The clouds winked down at him as if hinting at some ancient secret.

In May 1985, Leahy was the improbable leader of a Key West-based rock band known as the Overseas Highwaymen. The group was riding a wave of popularity in the South Florida music scene and gaining national recognition with their independently released album, *Margaritas at Sunset*. With a summer/fall tour beginning in a couple of months and several lucrative record deals pending,

Leahy should have felt on top of the world. Instead, he had a nagging feeling that pursuing fame and fortune wasn't what he should be doing.

He'd read the proposed contracts, perhaps more closely than any of his three bandmates. While rewarding on many levels, he viewed each deal as "a pair of golden handcuffs," and he urged the guys to remain autonomous and free of obligations to the corporate music world—even if that meant a smaller fan base, less money, and glory. Two of his bandmates believed they'd come to that once-in-a-career big break and thought it foolhardy not to take it.

In 1979, Andrew Leahy moved to the Florida Keys at age twenty-seven "to find himself and make a new start." Yet, he arrived in Key West with no plan for what he'd do or where he'd live. Initially, he worked in a series of tourist-oriented jobs and eventually found steadier employment with the Department of Transportation, which is where he met Gary Feld. Gary was an experienced bass player from the Buffalo, New York, area who moved to Florida to escape the harsh winters. Since Andrew had his six-string acoustic guitar and Gary played bass, they would meet after work and play together. After a time, they began playing in the local bars as a duo and called themselves the Overseas Highwaymen because they worked on the Overseas Highway, the roadway that runs through the Keys.

When nineteen-year-old keyboardist Billy Morris and twenty-year-old drummer Alan Browne joined them in 1984, the trajectory of the band changed. The addition of these two younger elite musicians turned the Overseas Highwaymen into a formidable musical force. Leahy and Feld were still working at the road department, but the time and energy necessary to sustain the vastly improved Overseas Highwaymen would eventually cause them to leave their day jobs.

As the band's main songwriter, Leahy composed songs with escapist themes, such as living a laid-back lifestyle, tropical locales, and having nonstop fun. While he may have considered some of these songs at odds with his serious and reflective personality,

Andrew realized he was no longer creating music for just himself. He was now a professional who had to appeal to a particular audience, and the consensus in the music industry was that Leahy was a talented songwriter.

As Leahy stood on the deck of his house with a thunderstorm looming on the horizon, his thoughts inevitably drifted back to his first day of classes at Millville College. He'd walked into his 8:00 a.m. English Composition class and sat across the aisle from a girl whose name he learned was Clare McGovern. She caught his attention from the outset. Her hair was the color of chestnuts, her eyes robin-egg blue. Side-swept bangs fell flatteringly across her oval-shaped face. A fading summer tan stressed her otherwise fair skin tone. None of this eluded the eighteen-year-old Leahy. Yet, although he could hardly overlook Clare's outward attractiveness, he sensed something about her that defied description, something that ran infinitely deeper than physical beauty.

Over their freshman year, Andrew and Clare became friends, good friends, nothing more—not on the surface anyway. Clare had a boyfriend she'd dated since high school and made it known at the start. Very little she'd ever done or said led him to believe they would ever have a more intimate bond. They spent most of their time at school together and often met off campus. For a while, Andrew attempted to teach Clare how to play the guitar, but these sessions always ended with Clare listening to Andrew playing his music.

Clare's favorite things to do with Andrew were kayaking on the bay and going out on the *Governor,* his dad's twenty-foot sailboat. Often they would go out around the lighthouse, drop anchor, and talk. Clare never told her boyfriend about these outings and called it a lie of omission. Early on, Andrew imagined this was an indication he might have a chance with her. Over time, however, he concluded he didn't and that Clare just enjoyed going out in the boat.

Whether it was under the guise of studying in the library, teaching Clare guitar in his basement, or being out on the water, every moment Andrew shared with her was precious.

One winter afternoon, after both had finished their schedule of classes, she offered to give him a ride to his car in a lot on the far side of campus. Snow was falling as they walked out of Turner Hall. Clare giggled and brushed her hands through the snowflakes that had landed on Andrew's head of light-brown hair. "Look," she said, "you have dandruff."

Andrew smiled and raised his hand to do the same to her. "So do you!" But the girl grabbed his hand and stopped him. For a lingering moment, their cold, wet fingers entwined until Clare finally released her grip, leaving the young man to wonder how to interpret her handholding. He hoped she meant to suggest the possibility of a deeper relationship.

Snow had accumulated by the time the two students reached Clare's '69 Chevy Nova. As Andrew cleared the windshield, he decided at that moment to place his heart on the line. He opened the passenger door and sat next to Clare, who had just turned the ignition to start the engine. "Can we talk for a few minutes?" he asked.

She adjusted the defroster to reduce the noise. "Sure," she said, "but I have to be at Jason's house by four-thirty."

The mention of Clare's boyfriend tore at Andrew's heart, and he hesitated. Maybe he'd be risking too much if he used the "L" word. She might respond by ending their friendship. Could he handle that? Not really. But what would the rest of his life be like if he didn't at least try? No one like Clare would ever come again. The characteristically shy young man meant to measure his words carefully. Andrew willed his voice to be steady. He wanted to touch her face, to embrace her, to give this moment the intimacy it deserved. Win, lose, or draw, he was about to create a lifetime memory. The sincerity in his voice was genuine.

"Clare, please listen."

"Have you seen the new James Bond movie?" she interrupted. "Jason and I are going to see it this weekend."

"No," Andrew said, "but what I'm trying to say is..."

She glanced at her watch. "Oh, I'm sorry. Can we do this later? Jason can be so impatient when I'm late."

Did Clare anticipate what he was about to say? Was she trying to avoid the topic?

Andrew turned his head and squeezed his eyes tightly, holding back the tears. After a slight hesitation, the words came pouring out of him like water over Niagara Falls. "This can't wait, Clare. You must know I like you, don't you? Well, it's more than that. It's *so* much more than that. I think of you every minute of every day. At night I lie awake with my eyes closed and see your face. I can hardly concentrate on schoolwork or just about anything else." Then he said it: "Clare, I love you."

Clare's demeanor softened, and her eyes searched Andrew's face. "I'm sorry," she said tenderly, "but I'm with Jason. You know that."

"I'm not trying to break you up with anyone. I only want you to understand." And it was true. Even as he'd opened the conversation, he'd known the best he could hope for was Clare's awareness of the exquisite nature of his feelings for her. He didn't expect her to plan their future together, and of this, he was correct.

Clare touched his hand. "We're friends, and I hope we'll always be friends. You're a great guy. You'll get over me and find someone, and when you do, she will be *very* lucky to have you. I mean it."

Andrew sighed, realizing Clare was being gentle. He locked his eyes on hers and said, "I don't think so. No matter how long I live, what I do, where I go, I'll never get over you."

Clare tried to lighten the mood. "Give it three weeks, tops," she said teasingly. "You'll get over me, and we won't let it spoil our friendship, okay?"

Three weeks?

No. Clare had been wrong, of course. Andrew hadn't gotten over her. And at this moment—fifteen years later—living alone in a house he had chosen for its isolation and proximity to the sea, Andrew's memories of Clare rose like the incoming tide. If only he could have one more chance to get through to her, he thought, just maybe his words would hit their mark.

2

CLARE

Monday, May 6, 1985
South Amboy, USA

At just after six o'clock in the morning, Clare Rinaldi slipped out from under the covers of her bed, careful not to awaken Sam, her fiancé. As she tiptoed to the en suite bathroom, she noticed soreness between her shoulder blades and stiffness in her neck. She'd had a persistent migraine for the past few days, and she felt abnormally tired—more tired than a healthy thirty-three-year-old woman should feel. Clare ignored her discomfort and attributed her present physical condition to the lingering effects of a presumed case of the flu she'd had three weeks earlier.

To feel better, she freshened up and put on the V-neck, floral-printed summer dress Sam liked so much. After doing her makeup and dabbing on some perfume, Clare headed downstairs to prepare Sam's breakfast, hoping he'd remember asking for a southwest omelet. If she prepared the *wrong* meal, he would turn the matter into an argument, but if he enjoyed his breakfast, he'd be nicer to her.

Clare wanted a successful marriage with Sam. Her previous marriage had failed when she'd caught her husband, Jason, having an affair with a trusted friend. Clare first met Sam shortly after she and Jason Rinaldi had separated, and she'd stopped into the South

Amboy Marina Café for lunch. When Sam noticed Clare was eating alone on the open-air deck overlooking the water, he stopped at her table to check on her. One word led to another, and soon they started seeing each other. Like Clare, Sam was going through a divorce. Moving in together was their chosen option until both were legally free to remarry.

Clare didn't regret jumping into another relationship so soon after separating from Jason. Ten years her senior, Sam represented the stability she believed she needed, so she overlooked petty grievances, such as leaving clothes on the hamper instead of in it and not putting the cap back on the toothpaste tube. To be sure, she had less patience with Sam's surliness and poor personal hygiene at home, and the handgun he kept on the top shelf of the bedroom closet was something else that made her uncomfortable. However, having grown up in over twenty foster homes, she tolerated things she could not control.

If Clare had to single out the one thing she resented most about Sam, it would be the idea that he'd insisted she resign from her teaching position at St. Ann High School to help run his restaurant. She'd worked hard to get her degree in secondary education from Millville College, and she had become a popular teacher with her history students at the local Catholic high school. Clare gave in when Sam offered to list her as the legal co-owner of the business, an arrangement that had so far failed to happen. The net effect was that she'd become an unpaid member of Sam's service staff.

For all of Sam's flaws, Clare had to give him credit for his ability to pull himself together when necessary. Each morning, Sam headed to the restaurant wearing a neatly pressed shirt and coordinated tie. He combed his well-oiled, slicked-back hair and carried himself with the pride of a successful business owner. In Clare's mind, Sam's demanding personality was necessary for him to succeed, so she made allowances for his less attractive traits.

She dialed the kitchen radio to her favorite music station, but within moments Clare heard a growling voice behind her. Setting out silverware and Sam's favorite coffee mug, Clare heard him say, "Hey, turn off that radio. I have a headache, and where's my coffee?"

Clare clicked the radio off and looked into Sam's bloodshot eyes. "Sit down, honey. Everything is ready. I just have to warm the milk so I can put it in your coffee."

"Good! I hate cold milk with my coffee. It makes the coffee"— Sam hesitated, as if trying to think of the right word—"cold...cold milk makes the coffee cold."

Clare removed a pot from the stovetop and poured some warm milk into Sam's mug. "Here's a hot cup of coffee. I hope you like it."

Sam took a sip and smiled. "That's good, really nice."

"Are you ready for your omelet?"

Sam squinted at her. "Didn't I tell you last night I wanted pancakes for breakfast?"

"No, honey. I'm sure you asked for a southwest omelet, but if you can hold on, I can whip up some pancakes."

"No, no, you're right. I asked for a southwest omelet. I remember now."

Clare slid a plate with the omelet and a piece of buttered toast in front of Sam. "Here you go!" She continued to stand next to him in case he asked for anything else.

Sam bit into the toast and said as he chewed, "I slept like a dead man. What time did you come to bed?"

"I stayed up reading until, I don't know, about midnight."

"Reading? What were you reading?"

"Oh, I was just flipping through some old cookbooks and looking for something different for us to eat today."

"Did you find anything interesting?" Sam asked while chewing.

"I found a recipe for herb-marinated rack of lamb. If you want that, I'll have to go to the store and buy some things. It takes thirteen hours to prepare."

"No, that's too expensive." He cleared his throat. "Anyway, I need you at the restaurant today. Come in around two this afternoon and cover for Lenore. She asked me to let her leave early."

"Sam, I'm sorry, but I don't feel up to it. I don't think I ever got over the flu last month."

Sam acted as if he didn't hear her. After a few more bites of the omelet, he put his fork down and lost interest in his food. "You look nice, Clare." He smiled and touched the folds of her dress. "Did you put this on for me?"

She knew she had to play along or face Sam's ire. "Maybe," Clare said, using that tone of coyness he always liked.

Sam stood up. "I'm sorry we argued last night." He moved closer and kissed her. His breath still smelled like booze from the night before, and the onions from the omelet did nothing to improve it.

Clare tried not to show her revulsion as she kissed him back. "I know you've been working hard lately, putting in all those hours." Her hands caressed his greasy hair. "I'm doing my best to keep you happy." She sniffled. "I'm just trying to be supportive. I only want to make you happy, but I can't figure out how to do that."

"Aw, baby." Sam again moved closer and embraced her. "You make me happy, most of the time anyway, but sometimes you forget. Promise me you won't forget anymore, and everything will be all right."

Clare nodded, but keeping Sam happy was not a simple task.

"Let's go upstairs."

"Not right now, Sam. I still have a headache."

Sam insisted, and in a few minutes, they were in bed and he was on top of her. That morning, however, Sam, still hung over from the night before, fell into another deep sleep.

Clare wiggled out from under her dead-to-the-world fiancé. She was certain Sam would snooze for at least another hour, so she returned to the kitchen and turned up the volume on the radio. Most of the time Sam did not like any extra noise in the house; therefore, playing the radio while she tidied up was a minor act of rebellion.

Minutes later, as she rinsed off some dishes in the sink, Clare sang along with a song on the radio. *Have you ever been in love? What am I supposed to say? Somehow all the things I'd been dreaming of got lost along the way.* Clare paused and considered the familiarity of the lyrics. *Andrew Leahy? Yes, that is Andrew!* Clare thought—the same Andrew Leahy who had been her close friend in college so many years ago. Clare remembered how Andrew had played that very song for her with just an acoustic guitar in an empty lecture hall.

As the music faded, the silky baritone voice of radio personality Ted Howard broke Clare's thought. "That's the second single off the debut album of the Overseas Highwaymen. Word is the Overseas Highwaymen will play summer dates in the Northeast. Once available, we'll have all the info right here."

Clare had never heard of the Overseas Highwaymen, but she was sure she recognized Andrew's vocals and the song's lyrics.

The slow thud-thud, thud-thud of Sam's feet descending the staircase caused Clare to turn off the radio. When Sam entered the kitchen, he was dressed for work, clean shaven, and in a fine mood. "Why did you turn off the radio? I was enjoying the song."

"Could you hear it from upstairs? I didn't mean to play it so loud."

"I could hear it from the landing. The song caught my ear, and I thought that poor fool of a singer will never have what we have, huh, Clare?"

3

LADY NADIA

1984
KEY WEST, FLORIDA

In January 1984, Andrew Leahy and Gary Feld were working full-time for the road department by day and moonlighting as the Overseas Highwaymen on evenings and weekends. They had even talked about leaving their day jobs to concentrate on music. If their employer would have given them a personal leave of absence, they would have been able to go back to their jobs. Unfortunately, the employer wouldn't approve a leave for that reason. Therefore, Leahy and Feld had to decide whether they should let go of the relative job security of a state job and risk the uncertainty of a music career. Guidance came from an unexpected source.

Leahy would often drive his red 1978 Jeep CJ-5 to Higgs Beach on Sunday afternoons. Routinely, he'd park his Jeep in the lot and walk along the beach to watch people or stroll out onto the pier to watch the water. On this day, the temperature was sixty-five degrees Fahrenheit, the sky was gray, and there was a stiff wind coming off the water. He imagined the tourists would think of this as a bad day, but the current weather was much to his liking—a good day for quiet contemplation.

He parked next to an ice cream truck and noticed a smartly

dressed woman in jeans and a sheer, light-blue blouse paying for a vanilla ice-cream cone. A few strands of the woman's braided jet-black hair fell elegantly across her face. When she turned to grab some napkins, she caught Andrew observing her. He nodded as he exited the Jeep with a jacket draped over his arm.

Andrew headed toward the pier, allowing the persistent sea breezes to swab his face. The ground beneath his feet shifted from beach sand to wooden planks once he stepped onto the pier, where he stopped and closed his eyes. This brought him back to childhood when he had gleefully smashed a sandcastle before the incoming waves could do it for him. In his mind's ear, he could hear his late father laugh and say, "The weather is changing. Come on, let's pack up and go home."

Andrew heard a woman's voice, and he reopened his eyes. "You like the wind, don't you?"

Her presence surprised him. "You like vanilla ice cream, don't you?" It wasn't the best comeback.

"I'm Robin."

"Robin?"

"That's right, Robin Karoly."

"Well, Robin Karoly, you have some ice cream on the side of your mouth." "Oh, do I?" She wiped both sides of her face with a paper napkin. "Better?"

Andrew nodded and introduced himself. "Andrew, Andrew Leahy."

"Nice to meet you Andrew, Andrew Leahy."

He met her mischievous gaze, exploring the woman's hazel eyes. Her lashes were long and black, and when she smiled, he smiled back. "Call me Andrew."

"Are you vacationing here in Key West, Mr. Leahy?"

"No, I live in the Keys, but I'm originally from somewhere else."

Robin took a bite of her cone. "Aren't most of us from somewhere else?"

"I suppose you're right. Many people come here because they think it's a chance to start a new life in paradise."

"Does that apply to you, Mr. Leahy?"

"It does."

Robin nodded toward the pier. "If you're walking out there, do you mind if I join you?"

Andrew again filled his lungs with cool salty air and regarded the wooden structure jutting toward the sea before giving his assent. "I'd enjoy the company."

Andrew and Robin were the only two people on the pier, and they slipped into an awkward silence until they reached the pier's halfway point. A strong wind-driven wave washed onto the pier and assailed their bodies. Andrew noticed Robin was shivering. "That's a beautiful blouse you're wearing, but it's not going to insulate you from today's weather out here on the pier. Why don't you slip on my windbreaker?"

Robin did so gratefully. "I wish I hadn't bought this ice cream. It's only making me colder."

"We can turn back if you're too cold. Let me walk you to your car."

Robin had to raise her voice above the wind. "Oh, I didn't drive here. I have a place off Duval Street, so I walked here thinking the sun would come out and the day would warm up. I'm such an optimist. Just walk with me to the end of the pier."

As they did so, Andrew told Robin how he'd come to Key West while alone on vacation. "I liked it so much that I moved here."

"How long have you been in the Keys?"

"About five years. I moved here in 1979. At first, I worked in several tourist-oriented jobs. Eventually, I got a job with the Department of Transportation."

"Where are you from originally?"

"It's a small town called South Amboy. I was an adult, living at home, and making money by giving music lessons in my parents' basement. I enjoyed doing that, but I didn't have many students, and it wasn't all that lucrative. So I moved here because I thought a change of scenery would be good."

"Are you still working for the Department of Transportation?" Robin asked as they reached the end of the pier.

"Yes, but I'm considering a new direction."

"Maybe you came here today hoping you'd get some time alone to think about it."

"Wow! You *are* perceptive."

"I'm sorry if I interrupted your reflection."

"You aren't. I'm enjoying your company."

As they turned around to walk back toward the beach, the light mist turned into a steady patter and then to a hard rain. By the time Andrew and Robin scurried to the shelter of his Jeep, both were soaking wet.

"I can't let you walk home in this. I'll give you a lift."

Robin agreed. "Normally, I wouldn't accept a ride from a stranger, but I'd appreciate that. Thank you. I'll need time to dry out before my six o'clock appointment."

During the ten-minute drive, Andrew continued to tell her about the career decision he faced. "When I started working with the road department, I met Gary. It just so happened he played bass guitar and I played a six-string acoustic guitar."

"That's right," Robin said. "You were teaching guitar back in South Amboy. You're a musician."

Andrew nodded. "Gary and I started playing together just for fun at first, but now we are getting paying jobs and calling ourselves the Overseas Highwaymen."

"Aha! So-called because of your jobs?"

"That's right! Making extra money doesn't hurt, but we were doing it for the sake of the music. A couple of months ago, we picked up two elite musicians, and the Overseas Highwaymen went from a duo to a four-piece band. We've been getting a lot more work, and neither Gary nor I can continue to keep up this pace if we still have to get up in the morning for work. We're both thinking of leaving the road department."

"What's stopping you?"

"I'd be giving up a steady job and a certain amount of job security, and I'm no kid anymore. Maybe if I were in my early twenties and working in a burger joint, it'd be worth a shot—nothing to lose, you know. These two new guys are fantastic, high level, but they are so young. Their future is undoubtedly in music. Billy Morris is just nineteen; he's the keyboardist. Alan Browne is twenty and plays any percussion instrument you can think of—steel drum, congas, marimbas, and vibes."

"If they're so good, why should their youth be such a concern?"

"To me, it's a maturity issue. This kid, Alan, is a bit of a hothead and wants to control things. He's got his ideas of how to play this, that, or the other thing. I'm not so hardheaded, and I think I know the art of compromise, but the songs are mine. We do a few covers, but I write most of what we play."

"You think they should play *your* music *your* way," Robin said, finishing Andrew's thought. "It sounds to me as if you're having some creative differences. Maybe everyone needs better-defined roles."

"We should address all that before I leave my job and commit full-time to the band."

"What kind of music do you do?"

"Gary and I had been playing classic rock, but now that we've grown into a professional band, we're developing more of an island sound—tropical rock, if you're familiar with that."

Robin pointed. "That's my place on the left. You can park in the driveway."

Even in the rain, Robin's aqua-blue home looked picture perfect. He read the sign on the white picket fence, *Lady Nadia, Psychic Consultant by Appointment,* and shot an inquiring glance at his passenger.

Robin chuckled. "Well, you've been telling me about yourself, but you never asked what I do."

"Is that you? Are you Lady Nadia?"

"Yes, but Robin is my real name. Lady Nadia is my professional name."

Andrew needed a few moments to digest the concept. "I guess *Lady Robin* doesn't have quite the same ring to it. You're a psychic, huh?"

"Why don't you come in? I'll get you a towel, and I can throw that wet shirt in the dryer and find something for you to wear while it dries."

Andrew had no experience with psychics, but unconsciously, he harbored a negative feeling toward them. He had no tolerance for trickery, and he believed psychics based their entire operation on deception. Yet, it was difficult to see Robin as a swindler interested in separating Key West tourists from their hard-earned money.

Once inside, Robin found Andrew a suitable T-shirt to wear while his shirt tumbled around in the dryer. She made them each a cup of tea, which they drank while sitting at an old-fashioned mahogany kitchen table.

"Is your six o'clock appointment for a psychic reading?"

"That's right, but I still have some time. You don't have to rush off."

"Can you tell me a little about what you do?"

Robin nodded as if Andrew's curiosity did not surprise her. "I don't predict the future, and I don't talk to the dead."

"And you don't predict the weather!"

"That's right. I'm a relationship psychic. My clients come to me with questions about whether they should stay in a relationship; they ask about cheating spouses or whether wedding bells are going to ring."

"Can you answer those questions?"

"I sense streams of psychic energy or impressions, and this allows me to counsel my clients on matters of the heart."

Andrew shook his head. "I don't get it. How do you do that?"

"Try this. Close your eyes."

Andrew did as she asked him to do.

Robin continued, "I'm going to say a word that represents an object, and I want you to create an image of that object in your mind."

Andrew agreed. "Okay."

"Apple!"

Andrew visualized an apple.

"What do you see?"

"I'm picturing an apple."

"What color?"

"It's red, but not shiny like you'd see in a supermarket. It reminds me of the apples grown on a farm on the outskirts of my hometown."

"Imagine you're taking a bite of the apple. How does it taste?"

"When I chew, it's sweet. The juice drips down my chin."

"Open your eyes. Did you just eat an apple?"

"No, I only imagined it."

"Well, that's the best way I can describe to you what I do. It's a matter of getting an impression. You got the impression of eating an apple, but you didn't physically eat an apple."

Andrew remained skeptical. "What's love got to do with the visualization of an apple?"

Robin let the question hang between them for a moment. "Much like your imaginary apple, love exists more on a spiritual rather than a physical level. Loving someone is an intense, mystical experience. I can often sense that level of intensity."

Although Andrew didn't understand, he said, "I see."

"It's interesting, however, that when some people come to me and say they want a romantic relationship, they habitually do everything they can to avoid it. They lack the spiritual skill necessary for such a deep connection. My gift is that I can see beyond the veil imposed by the conventions of the physical world. I show people that the genuine nature of relationships is not physical or materialistic. It's spiritual."

"Is it possible Lady Nadia just has a knack for reading people? Maybe there are no actual psychic abilities involved."

Robin's response didn't answer his suggestion directly, but it convinced Andrew she was an intuitive person. "People often only want superficial relief from the suffering of the external world. To be worthy of true love, there has to be certain enlightenment."

Andrew understood what Robin meant. He would never be the same person he'd been before meeting Clare. Clare had shaped his worldview and established the way he lived his life.

Robin glanced at her watch. "Excuse me while I check if your shirt has dried." She stepped out of the kitchen. When she returned, Andrew was rinsing off the cups in the sink. "Thanks, I could have gotten that."

"How's my shirt?"

Robin handed Andrew his shirt. "I'm afraid it's still a little damp. I'm also afraid I have to ask you to leave now, so why don't you wear the one you have on. You can keep it, or you can bring it back when you're in the neighborhood."

"Okay, but I should bring the shirt back. I'd *like* to bring it back. I wish I could have stayed longer. We were having such an interesting conversation."

Robin stopped Andrew before he left. "There's one more thing I'd like you to do for me. Close your eyes."

"Close my eyes? Am I visualizing more apples?"

"*Shhh!* Just do it!"

"Okay, okay, I'm closing my eyes."

Robin held Andrew's hands. "I'm closing my eyes as well." After a few meditative breaths, she said, "If you pursue a music career, you will experience extraordinary success and will become a nationally celebrated musician. The music is only a vehicle for something else and may have to be scaled back at some point. Music will always be a part of who you are; however, you may have to give up fame and adoration for something or someone more important."

Andrew opened his right eye just enough to see Robin's face. "What does that mean?"

She let go of his hands. "The Universe is not ready to reveal anything more, but the Universe is preparing you for reorganization."

"What do you mean by *reorganization*? Like when a corporation reorganizes, like a shake-up?"

"I like that!" Robin laughed. "Yes, a shake-up. You might also think of it as a midcourse correction."

"Can you be a little more specific?"

"I'm afraid not, but follow your music. It will take you where you need to go."

4

A TRANSFORMATIVE EXPERIENCE

C lare felt a sudden wave of nausea and headache, but she didn't have enough time to reach the toilet bowl in the half bath before her stomach contracted so forcefully that the contents propelled and splattered onto the tile floor. She sank to her knees and heaved until only clear mucus came up.

Feeling weak, she recovered and got up from the floor, careful not to step into her vomit. There was no one else to clean up the mess, but before turning her attention to that task, she went to the kitchen sink and ran some cool water to soothe her throat, irritated by stomach acid.

That morning she was too sick to work, but Sam insisted. With her head feeling as if someone was shooting lightning bolts into her brain, she doubted she could go to the restaurant under any circumstances. After resting for an hour, the queasiness passed and the headache subsided, so she fortified herself with a cup of clear chicken broth, dressed in her fuchsia and green uniform with matching apron, and drove to the restaurant.

For the first ninety minutes, she was glad she had forced herself to work. It was a bright sunny day, and she enjoyed serving patrons on the veranda. One of her customers was a bearded man who smiled and nodded at Clare each time she passed his table.

Clare presented the man with a menu and filled his water glass. "I'm Clare. I'll be taking care of you. Would you like to look over the menu?"

"I'm ready to order. May I have the shrimp scampi?"

Clare jotted the order on her pad. "It comes with a side salad. What kind of dressing?"

"May I have red wine vinaigrette, please?"

"If there's nothing else, I'll put your order right in."

In response, the man stood, towering over her. "Thank you."

His scraggly beard obscured most of his facial features. She wondered if this guy was from a foreign culture. Such formality was unnecessary in a place where Sam stressed a casual dining experience. "Sit down and relax. Your order will be right out."

The peculiar man remained on his feet. "Excuse me, Clare."

"Yes."

"May I say something?"

Several male customers had flirted with her the past few weeks. These overtures had not escaped Sam's notice. Given this experience, Clare assumed he was about to ask her for a date; she didn't have a spare minute to rebuff his advances and needed to keep working. She sounded more abrupt than she'd intended. "Sorry, but I'm engaged. I'm engaged to the owner of the restaurant, so I can't go out with you. Let me just put your order in."

He shook his head and suppressed a chuckle. "Oh no, that's not it."

Clare flushed, feeling embarrassed that she had expected the man's question without giving him a chance to ask it. "How may I help you?"

The man tugged on his beard. "I feel by your presence you are going to have a transformative experience."

"Oh, I see. If you're a salesperson..."

This time, the man could not contain his amusement and laughed openly. "Am I a salesperson? I should say no. You may think of me as a messenger, perhaps, but I'm not selling anything." He paused as if waiting for eye contact, and his voice took a serious tone. "I don't blame you if you find me impertinent, but I *feel* as if you are about to have a life-changing experience, one that will bring you many insights."

Clare half expected the man to hand her a fortune cookie. "What kind of experience, and how do you know this?"

"I *feel* it—through intuition, if you will." He smiled at Clare in an almost paternal way. "When it happens, do not be afraid."

"If you'll pardon me, I've got to get your order in, and there are other customers, so if you'll excuse me..." Clare effectively ended the discussion.

"Of course," he said, finally taking his seat.

Mr. Fortune Cookie, as Clare thought of him, made her uncomfortable. It relieved her when the strange fellow simply ate his meal, paid his bill, and left a modest tip before leaving the restaurant without additional conversation.

As her shift proceeded into the evening, Clare's headache returned with a vengeance, and her mouth and lips felt abnormally dry. The fever was back, and she realized she had probably become dehydrated. It took every ounce of energy to keep working when all she wanted to do was to go home and rest in bed.

Grateful that it was getting close to closing time, Clare offered the dessert menu to a young couple sitting at a corner table. The man and woman held hands, and Clare noticed rings on their fingers. The pair reminded Clare of how she'd once been. That was before—before she'd seen through the illusion of romantic love. She wanted to take the young woman aside and tell her *it wasn't real*. Instead, she asked, "Would you like dessert?"

"Thank you," the man said. "Let's look."

Clare noted the gentleness in his smile and the softness in his eyes, which in some small measure gave her hope that love really did exist. "The twisted strawberry shortcake is our newest dessert item. I haven't tried it yet, but it looks very good. It's a citrus angel food cake, layered with strawberries, pudding, and white chocolate."

"Hmm, it sounds good," the woman said. "Can we split one order?"

Clare smiled. "Sure, I'll bring an extra plate."

Clare was mindful that her cynical view of love originated from life experience. From what little information she knew, her mother put her up for adoption as a newborn. For the first fourteen years of her life, Clare moved from one foster home to another and developed no close ties along the way. At age seven, life stabilized to a degree when the Stevenson family took her in. Mr. and Mrs. Stevenson served as her foster parents until Clare turned fourteen, but they had other foster children in their home as well. These children were little more than roommates, and Clare felt no particular closeness to them or her foster parents.

Her view of romantic love took a more favorable, though temporary, turn in high school when she started dating Jason. As high school sweethearts, Clare and Jason were all but inseparable. Even when the couple attended separate colleges, Clare assumed she and Jason would get married once they finished their education, which indeed turned out to be the case.

Throughout high school and college, Clare had remained faithful to Jason; however, there was this one guy she'd met at Millville College named Andrew. Andrew was popular on campus because he often played his guitar out on the lawn when the weather was nice. Such impromptu sessions often attracted a crowd eager to sing along.

By the second week of classes, Clare welcomed Andrew as a new friend, but she could tell he wanted to be more than friends. For the sake of her relationship with Jason, Clare hid her feelings for Andrew from everyone, including herself. Maybe if Andrew had tried a little harder, the young music major could have made her forget about Jason. Clare and Andrew stayed friends throughout their four years at Millville. During the summer after graduation, Clare heard from Andrew several times by telephone, but she never saw him again, eventually losing contact altogether.

After marrying Jason, the additional pieces of her life began falling into place when she landed her first teaching job at a Catholic high school in the nearby town of South Amboy. Jason started working for the telephone company.

As a new teacher, Clare welcomed the mentorship of Janine Delacruz, who had been teaching tenth grade social studies for the past two years. Clare and Janine became good friends outside of work, and Jason and Janine hit it off as well. Clare suspected nothing when Jason and Janine began shopping together at the local flea market every Saturday morning. It all seemed innocent enough until the afternoon Clare found a sexy, lace-trimmed thong panty in between the sheets of her unmade bed.

Clare confronted Jason that same evening, but he denied any knowledge of the undergarment and couldn't explain the unmade bed in the middle of the day. "The panty must be yours, and maybe you just forgot to make the bed this morning."

"I know it isn't mine," Clare said emphatically. "It's too big, and I know what's mine and what isn't!"

After a long silence, Jason confessed while avoiding eye contact with Clare. "It's Janine's. We've been seeing each other."

"You slept with my friend in my bed? Just get out! Get out! Go on and get the hell out?"

While her divorce from Jason was pending, she'd stopped at South Amboy Marina Café for a bite to eat after hearing rave reviews from some of the other teachers at her school. It was there she met the owner, Sam, who had recently taken over the business from his parents. Sam was ten years older than Clare and represented more maturity and stability than Jason. Like Clare, Sam was going through a divorce and was open to the possibility of a second chance at marriage. Clare and Sam considered themselves to be an engaged couple as they awaited their final divorce decrees.

Shortly after Sam proposed, he told Clare he wanted to expand the dining room. Clare hardly gave it a second thought when he asked her to invest all of her savings in the renovation project. After all, Sam had promised Clare they would see a return on that investment "in no time." Clare knew little about the restaurant business, yet she accepted Sam's view that it would all work out.

Lately, however, minor disagreements had popped up. Often, these had to do with what Sam perceived as the extra attention Clare gave to male customers. Sam had also complained that Clare was a poor housekeeper at home. Worst of all, Sam started drinking. At first, the drinking seemed like nothing—a glass or two of wine in the evening. But then he turned to hard liquor and started drinking earlier in the day. Clare remained naive to what was happening until she noticed Sam's shakiness and grouchiness in the mornings. Once she realized Sam needed a drink simply to quell these early morning shakes, she expressed her concern, and Sam didn't like it when Clare expressed her concern. No, he didn't like it at all.

Clare pushed these thoughts out of her mind and served the strawberry shortcake to her young customers. "Here you go!"

"It looks like the restaurant is getting ready to close," the young man said. "I hope we'll have time to enjoy this."

Although Clare was feeling deathly ill, she projected positivity and told the couple to take their time. "We still have some tidying up to do, and we're getting ready for tomorrow. Enjoy your dessert and tell me how you like it."

As Clare passed the outdoor table where the earlier customer had eaten his shrimp dinner, she noticed a dark-blue umbrella left behind. It was odd for anyone to carry an umbrella on such a sparkling, cloudless day. She tried to remember if any other customer had been there after him but didn't think so. Clare took the item to the restaurant's lost-and-found closet in the back of the kitchen.

After shutting the closet door, Clare headed back to the dining area, but she stopped in the middle of the kitchen and began sweating profusely. The kitchen lights hurt her eyes, and she found the clanging sound of pots and pans to be intolerable. The pain in her head worsened again. She was light-headed now as well, and this made it difficult to think. Clare looked around for a chair or something else to sit on, but her strength was so diminished that all she could do was descend to the floor.

In her fading awareness, she could hear someone saying, "Clare is on the floor. Call an ambulance!" Clare tried to hold on, but the shroud of unconsciousness descended upon her.

5

THE HOSPITAL AND BEYOND

From Clare's point of view, it was as if some inexplicable force transferred her to a hospital where two doctors and a nurse were attending to a patient. The nurse said, "According to her boyfriend, she was near the end of her shift at a restaurant when someone found her collapsed on the kitchen floor. She was lethargic in the ambulance, slipping in and out of consciousness."

When Clare heard that, she thought it sounded a lot like her day. She had a fuzzy recollection of someone saying she needed to get to the hospital, and she remembered being lifted into an ambulance. *Funny*, she thought, *because I feel much better now.*

The taller doctor turned around and faced her. As he did so, she could see that *she* was the patient on the bed, still dressed in her fuchsia and green uniform. "Do not be afraid," the doctor said. She had heard these words from the weird customer back at the restaurant.

Clare stepped closer to get a better look. "That's me, but it can't be because I'm over here, and I'm not sick anymore."

"They can't hear or see you, Clare," the taller doctor said.

The stranger customer, Clare thought. She glanced at his nametag: Dr. Jerome Emiliani.

"What do you mean? Why can't they see me?"

"They can't see me either, but that's not important right now—"

Clare interrupted in a tone of panic. "I'm dead! That's it, isn't it?

I'm dead!" She turned to the nurse. "Excuse me! Can someone tell me what's happening here?"

When neither the nurse nor the other doctor responded, Dr. Emiliani repeated, "As I say, they can't see or hear you, but there's no need for concern."

"But you can see me, so why can't they? Am I dead or what?"

Next, Clare heard the other doctor mention an order for blood work. "I'm *not* dead. Otherwise, why would they be doing blood work, right?"

Dr. Emiliani tugged on his facial hair. "I think you're catching on!"

"Catching on? I'm totally confused."

"The doctors will run blood tests, brain scans, and collect cerebrospinal fluid. The diagnosis will be bacterial meningitis. Your body is comatose."

"They haven't even run the tests yet! How do you know the results? Either I'm critically ill, or I'm having a very vivid hallucination, or both."

"Your body exists in the world of form and is vulnerable to critical illness. Medical doctors serve the physical world; therefore, they deal with matters that are science-orientated, but the human body is just an encasement. The real Clare is not the physical body on the bed. The real Clare is her spirit."

"Who *are* you?"

"My role is to facilitate your experience here in the realm of spirit. You may call me Jerome."

"Am I going to die?"

"Death is merely an illusion," Jerome said, smiling in the same paternal way Clare remembered from the restaurant. "If you're asking if your body will die because of this illness, that's a question for which I have no answer."

Fascinated, Clare stared at her physical body. "What happens next?"

Hearing no answer, she turned to see Dr. Emiliani was no longer there. Clare convinced herself she was having a weird, though vivid, dream. This was some measure of comfort because she assumed that she would eventually wake up.

In her mind's ear, she heard Dr. Emiliani's voice. *No, Clare. This is not a dream, and you have work to do.*

Clare glanced around, thinking Dr. Emiliani had returned, but he was not there. She turned her attention to the other emergency room physician who was still examining her body. "I have bacterial meningitis. What is bacterial meningitis?"

She reached for the curtain, thinking she should find someone who could see and hear her. If she could convey Dr. Emiliani's diagnosis, the medical staff could treat her sooner and hasten her recovery. When she touched the curtain, Clare's hand passed through it. She pulled her hand back and saw it had a translucent quality about it.

The doctor instructed the nurse, but Clare couldn't quite catch his words.

The nurse said, "Yes, Dr. Youngman, right away," and she opened the curtain and rushed out through an open door.

Clare followed and watched the nurse sprint down the hallway, around a corner, and out of sight. Meanwhile, Clare noticed a portly security guard dawdling toward her, but she could not attract his attention either. Next, she poked her head in a waiting area a few doors away, where she discovered Sam sitting alone and assumed he must be waiting for some news about her.

She yelled his name. "Sam!" But he merely checked his watch and sighed impatiently.

Failing to communicate with Sam, Clare wandered about the emergency department looking for Dr. Emiliani. After all, hadn't he said something about facilitating her experience in the spirit realm? Well, she would welcome some guidance right now.

Clare approached the nurse's station. "Excuse me, will someone page Dr. Emiliani?" Just then, she realized Emiliani probably didn't work for the hospital. Maybe someone else, some higher power, had engaged him.

If this wasn't a conventional dream, what was happening to

her? Was she in some space between life and death? Is death an illusion, as Emiliani had said? And what did he mean when he said she had work to do? Her questions were too much to fathom.

For the moment, she abandoned any further attempts to communicate with the hospital staff. *This is frustratingly weird*, Clare thought. *I've got bacterial meningitis, and no one knows I'm out of my body.*

She returned to the room in which her body was being treated and found it filled with an impenetrable mist, and she could no longer see herself or anything from the hospital. There was nothing solid underfoot, and she couldn't discern any sense of right and left or up and down.

A moment later, the mist cleared, and Clare found herself on a predawn beach standing barefoot in knee-deep, temperate seawater. She became fascinated by how each wavelet broke upon the stone-laden shore, accepting its fate without complaint.

In the morning stillness, she inhaled the salty sea air and beheld the first ribbon of daylight just above the horizon. As the sun rose higher in the sky, the shadowy outline of rocks and vegetation became clearer. Clare wandered down the beach for maybe twenty yards until a lonesome house came into view. She wondered if any answers awaited her there.

6

UNEXPECTED GUEST

TUESDAY MORNING, MAY 7, 1985
LOWER SUGARLOAF KEY

By May 1985, it appeared as if Lady Nadia's prediction about Andrew's success was coming true. With "Margaritas at Sunset" climbing the national charts, and another song getting significant radio play, the Overseas Highwaymen were the hottest band in South Florida.

One unfortunate development was that a national tabloid had gotten the idea that rising rock star Andrew Leahy was dating "Key West's most gifted psychic," Lady Nadia. Another magazine reported that Lady Nadia had advised Leahy to quit his job at the Department of Transportation to facilitate his rise to stardom.

Things got out of hand when a Miami radio disc jockey called Leahy to verify the Lady Nadia story. Live on air, Andrew tried to evade the question; however, when the DJ pressed him, Andrew innocently admitted that the story was partially true. This created a firestorm of unwanted publicity, and nearly everyone associated with the Overseas Highwaymen feared this incident would hurt the band's rising popularity. Ironically, just the opposite occurred. The situation expanded the band's fan base and was most likely a factor in propelling "Margaritas at Sunset" to the top of the charts.

The media's attention had a less favorable impact on Robin. At first, she welcomed the spike in her psychic business, but the extraordinary publicity brought out too many kooks. Even though she billed herself as a relationship psychic, many of her new patrons demanded advice on how to achieve their fame and fortune, and Lady Nadia didn't have the gifts to deliver that service.

Robin telephoned Andrew before dawn to complain about how ridiculous things were getting. "Sorry if I woke you, but I couldn't sleep because of what the tabloids are saying. Did you see that one article suggesting I'm some sort of 'black magic priestess' and that I 'cast a spell' to ignite the band's success?"

Leahy rubbed his eyes and checked the clock. "Wow! That is absurd! I'm sorry you've gotten so caught up in this whole hullaballoo. Maybe once I leave for the summer tour, things will quiet down for you. Can I make it up to you by inviting you here for breakfast? We can talk more about it if you want to."

"You'll have to give me about ninety minutes. I can bring the eggs and bacon."

"Great! That will give me time to shower, dress, and put on a pot of coffee. Just come in. I'll leave the side door unlocked."

Just as the coffee brewed, the front door flung open, and Robin carried in some groceries. "Hey, have you seen that sunrise? Step out onto the deck with me."

Andrew appreciated his relationship with Robin. Although she was serious and intuitive at heart, she also had a playful, good-natured side to her personality. "Don't bother knocking. Just barge right in! Why don't you?"

Robin laughed. "Hey, leave the door open, and you never know what the wind will blow in." She grabbed Andrew's hand and dragged him out to the balcony while leaving the French doors open behind them. At this hour, darkness had already surrendered to an ethereal glow of sunlight in hues of tangerine and pink.

"You know, no matter how ugly life gets, the dawn of a new day should remind us there is beauty all around and within us if we'd only pay attention."

Before Andrew could agree, he heard a knock on the front door. "Wonder who that could be."

"What do you mean?"

"Someone is knocking."

"I hear nothing."

"There it is again," he said, walking back into the house.

When Andrew opened the door, he could hardly believe his eyes. *Clare?* At first, he thought she looked exactly as she did in college. Her clear blue eyes possessed the same electricity, and her chestnut-colored hair shimmered in the light of early morning. As he looked more closely, however, he noticed some refinement. Her face had lost the gentleness of youth and subtle lines appeared at the corners of her eyes, but Clare had matured into an astonishingly beautiful woman.

Clare's jaw dropped. "Andrew?"

"Yes," he said, still trying to recover from the shock of seeing Clare after so many years. "How did you know I lived here?"

"I didn't. I sort of got lost on the beach. Maybe I need directions or something. Your lights were on, so I knocked, but I didn't know you lived here."

"Well, come in. We're just about to have breakfast."

By this time, Robin entered the room. "Who was it?"

Andrew didn't understand the inquisitive look on Robin's face. "I'd like you to meet my old college classmate from Millville College. Robin, this is Clare McGovern. Clare, this is Robin."

"It's nice to meet you." Clare extended her hand.

"Andrew, you're such a practical joker!" Robin said. "There was nobody at the door."

"I love your sense of humor, Robin, but don't be rude."

Clare cleared her throat before uttering, "She can't see or hear me. It's just like at the hospital. No one could see or hear me there either, except Mr. Shrimp Scampi or, should I say, Dr. Emiliani?"

Andrew tried not to laugh. "What's Mr. Shrimp Scampi, an entrée or something?"

"Wait!" Robin exclaimed. "There's someone here. I feel a presence."

"Clare, did I forget to mention that Robin is better known as Lady Nadia, Key West's most gifted psychic?"

"Seriously, Andrew," Clare said, "psychic or not, she can't see or hear me. Yet, I feel a sense of connection with her."

"Follow me," Robin said, leading Andrew to the kitchen table.

Andrew rubbed his right temple. Oh sure, he'd imagined how a chance encounter would bring Clare back to him, and they'd ruminate about their college days. Finally, Andrew would find the words to tell Clare how he had thought of her every single day of his adult life, that no one else had ever come along who could remotely compare to her. Yes, he would use the "L" word. The other part of his fantasy was that Clare would have the depth of understanding to know Andrew's feelings were true. Instead, Clare appeared on Andrew's doorstep— invisible to his psychic friend—referring to Dr. Shrimp Scampi, or some such. No, this wasn't quite the reunion he'd imagined.

Robin pulled the kitchen chairs away from the table and said, "Let's sit and see if we can sort this all out, shall we?"

Clare didn't know quite where she was or why she was there, but when Andrew answered the door and looked at her with the same intensity, she felt as if something had clicked.

"But Robin," Andrew asked, "why can I see Clare and you can't?"

"That's the key question, isn't it? Is Clare still here?"

"I'm right in front of you."

"Yes," Andrew said. "She's here."

"Clare, tell us what happened to you. How did you get here? Do you know why you are here? What do you want? How can we help you?"

"I hardly know where to start," Clare said, knowing only Andrew could hear her. "It's all so overwhelming. Where am I exactly?"

"This is my house in the Florida Keys. Take your time. I will repeat what you say for Robin."

Clare explained that she lived with Sam and worked at his restaurant called South Amboy Marina Café and how she'd gone to work despite feeling sick because Sam was short-staffed and insisted he needed her.

"I felt better once I started working, at least for a little while. And then, I had this mysterious customer. He was very tall with a long beard, and he had this formal way of speaking. He told me I was going to have a 'transformative experience' and that I shouldn't be afraid when it happens."

Andrew repeated what Clare said.

"And what happened next?" Robin asked.

Clare said the man caused her discomfort, so all she wanted to do was take the customer's order and step away from him. "In my mind, I started thinking of him as Mr. Fortune Cookie and Mr. Shrimp Scampi, but later in the hospital, when I saw his name tag, I knew him as Dr. Jerome Emiliani."

"So, this customer is a doctor?" Andrew asked.

"That's what his name tag said."

Clare shrugged. "At closing time, I started feeling ill again. Next, I remember the feeling of blacking out in the kitchen. I must have been in and out of consciousness during the ambulance ride. I don't remember any of it. The next thing I can recall is that I was at the hospital standing next to a stretcher, and there were two doctors and a nurse with a patient. The patient on the table was me. I was both the patient and the observer."

Clare's eyes wandered to Andrew's. "Dr. Emiliani was the only one who could see or hear me at the hospital. I couldn't communicate with any other staff. I found Sam in a waiting area, but he couldn't see me either. Dr. Emiliani told me I had bacterial meningitis even before the staff had run any tests or lab work."

"The customer from the restaurant must be the key to all this. What do you think, Robin?" Andrew asked.

"I doubt it. No, I think he must be a guide for Clare, but he's not the key. Maybe you're the key, Andrew."

"Me? What makes you say that?"

Robin stood up and poured herself a cup of orange juice from Andrew's refrigerator. Before taking her first sip, she said, "You are the only one who can see and hear Clare in the physical world. Don't you get it? There has to be a reason for that."

"What about this so-called *doctor*?" Andrew asked. "He could see her in the physical world."

"I don't believe he's from the physical world. He appeared as Clare's customer; he spoke to her before she passed out in the kitchen, and he was at her bedside in the hospital, but I think his purpose is to give Clare some sort of direction."

Andrew turned to Clare. "Did anyone else at the restaurant check on his table or serve Emiliani anything?"

"I was very sick for the entire shift. Maybe someone saw him or maybe not. I probably wasn't thinking straight."

"And you say none of the hospital staff seemed to acknowledge him?"

"I don't think anyone in the hospital could see him except me."

Andrew turned to Robin. "Well, Emiliani hasn't made his presence known to anyone except Clare. What do you make of that?"

"If he's a spirit guide, he can probably do whatever is necessary to accomplish his assignment."

Clare leaned into Andrew and whispered, "What does she mean by *assignment*?"

"What do you think *is* his assignment?" Andrew asked, rephrasing Clare's question.

"This is all speculation, but even though I think you have some key role to play in all this, Emiliani must be working with Clare. Honestly, this situation is beyond my field of expertise. I've encountered nothing like this before. I mean, spirit guide, out-of-body experience...I usually advise people on their love lives..." Robin's voice trailed off as if considering a new possibility.

"What?" Andrew asked.

"Your aura is lighting up like the lights on Broadway!"

Andrew frowned. "What does Broadway have to do with any of this?"

Robin shook her head. "It's just an expression." She inspected Andrew up and down. "Tell me how you know Clare."

"We were friends throughout college," Andrew said, "but we lost touch, and I haven't seen her since graduation."

"Did you have a dating relationship?"

"No, Robin, not a boyfriend-girlfriend relationship. It wasn't like that. We studied together, ate together, and helped each other through the four years."

"I'm certain you had some feelings for her, powerful feelings. I couldn't sense that before, but I can sense it now."

"She had a steady boyfriend. His name was Jason. No, Clare and I were never in a dating relationship."

Clare finally spoke. "Excuse me, but you're talking as if I'm not even here."

"We're not ignoring you," Andrew said. "We're just trying to figure this out."

"This is going to take a lot of my psychic energy," Robin said, "but I want to try reading you again, Andrew."

Andrew chuckled. "You can't read me. You've tried several times, but as you say, my armor is impenetrable."

"You do put up a strong front, but with Clare here, your walls are weaker. Give me some space to gather my psychic strength. I have to meditate for a while, Andrew. Maybe you'd like to take Clare out on the deck and get reacquainted."

Andrew and Clare walked onto the deck, standing side by side in the sunlight of a warm Florida morning. When Clare spoke, it wasn't about her current predicament. "I've heard your music on the radio. I'm happy you're so successful."

"Thanks. I came to the Keys in 1979 because things weren't happening back home. I got a steady job with the road department, but I was also playing music at night. Robin advised me to pursue music and give up my day job. She predicted my music career would flourish, and that prediction has come true."

"Are you guys together?"

"No, we're just friends. We're not dating or living together. Today she came over for breakfast because of some not-so-accurate stuff that's come out in the press, and she wanted to talk about it."

"Do you think she can help me?"

"I don't know, but Robin has some unusual talents."

"Shouldn't I get back to my body?"

"Maybe, but let's see what Robin comes up with."

"You know, Andrew, I always wondered if I would ever see you again."

Andrew smiled wistfully. "I've wondered the same thing about you."

"If you're curious, I married Jason right after graduation and got a teaching job at St. Ann's High School."

"I don't understand. Who's Sam?"

"Jason and I are divorcing. I'm engaged to Sam now."

"Oh?"

"Jason was unfaithful."

"I'm sorry. I know you were with Jason since high school and throughout college."

"I met Sam soon after separating from Jason. Sam convinced me to give up my teaching job and work in his restaurant, which he'd recently taken over from his parents. We're getting married once our divorces are final—that is, if I come out of this coma."

"Oh yeah," Andrew said, "the coma." He motioned for Clare to follow him back into the house where his psychic friend had prepared breakfast. "Let's hear what Robin has to say." He waited while Clare stopped to take one last look at the view from the deck.

Suddenly, she became enveloped by a mysterious mist and disappeared.

7

ANDREW'S TRUTH

Andrew called to Robin, "Clare's gone!"

Robin joined Andrew out on the deck. "What are you talking about? Where did she go?"

Andrew tried to explain what he had just witnessed. "This strange fog surrounded Clare, and she just vanished."

Robin closed her eyes. "I don't feel her presence anymore. She's moved on."

"Moved on? Do you mean her physical body has died, and her spirit has moved on to wherever the spirit goes once it leaves the earthly existence?"

Robin shrugged. "Again, I'm out of my field of expertise, but it is significant Clare came to you. Would you like to tell me about your relationship with Clare?"

At first, Andrew tried to protect his secret. "We were friends in college. I haven't seen her since graduation."

Robin motioned. "Let's sit in the kitchen. There's more to this story than you're telling me. I can sense that much."

"Maybe we are having a joint hallucination. Like I saw someone who wasn't there, and you bought into it."

Robin shook her head. "No, someone's spirit was here, and I need you to be forthcoming unless you don't care to figure this out."

"Okay." It was time for Andrew to let down his defenses. "I

guess you could say I had feelings for her." He smiled at how his words—*had feelings for her*—minimized the true depth of it. "Clare had a boyfriend from high school, so as I've said, we weren't boyfriend and girlfriend."

"Did you ever tell her about your feelings?"

"I tried, but it was so hard for me."

"What do you mean?"

"I was shy, and I kept my feelings to myself until I thought I would burst, but yeah, I once tried to tell her."

"How did that go?"

"I knew nothing I could say would change anything," Andrew said. "Yet, I needed her to know how I felt, so I told her I loved her."

"How did she respond to you?"

"She tried to be nice about it, but it still hurt like hell to be rejected. That was freshman year. We kept our friendship intact through four years of college, but after graduation, she dropped out of my life. I never saw Clare again until she showed up here this morning."

"Maybe there is some unfinished business."

Andrew still harbored an undeniable need to tell Clare how he felt about her. "When I told her, I never believed my words truly hit their mark. Maybe Clare understood, but I never got the sense she did. Or maybe she understood on an intellectual level, but I don't think she understood in her heart."

"How did you feel seeing her today?"

"Dumbstruck at first," he said. "Overall, I thought she had become a beautiful woman."

"No!" Robin reproved. "I didn't ask you what you thought. I asked how you felt. We're dealing with the spirit realm here—not the physical or material world. How did you *feel* seeing her again?"

"I felt like the very first instant I saw her. Nothing changed."

"Love at first sight?" Robin asked in a gentle tone.

"Not everyone believes in love at first sight."

"What about you?"

"I've had fifteen years to think about Clare. As I turned it over in my mind, I'd wonder if love at first sight is just a physical or sexual attraction. How could I be in love with someone I'd never dated? Sure, we'd done things outside of school, but there were never any dates."

"Have you thought about her a lot over the years?"

Andrew stared straight ahead. "I've thought of Clare every day of my adult life. As I said, we never dated."

"Activities are not the same as emotions," Robin said. "Many people who go through the motions of dating are not in love with each other. Or, a person could be in love with another and never dated."

"The love I feel for Clare just *is*. Maybe I can't explain or justify it. It just *is*." He stood up from the table and reached for the telephone on the kitchen wall.

"Who are you calling?"

"I've got to know if Clare is still alive. I need the numbers for some of the area hospitals. If I can find out what hospital she's in, maybe I'll find out what's going on with her."

"A hospital may not release any information to you over the phone. You're not a relative, and they don't know you."

"While we were on the deck, Clare said something about working at South Amboy Marina Café. I'm familiar with the place, and Clare told me she lives with the owner. Maybe if I call the restaurant, someone there will tell me something."

After tracking down the telephone number of the café, Andrew placed the call, but he only got a recorded message saying the restaurant didn't open until eleven o'clock in the morning. It frustrated him to have to wait a few more hours. "They must do lunch and dinner only."

"In the meantime, maybe Clare will reappear."

"Maybe she passed away, and I'll never see her again."

Robin shook her head. "Physical bodies live and die, but if your love for Clare is true, it exists forever. I've known people who have split up, divorced, and married other people, yet they remained bound in love. The world's conventions don't matter. You will see her again someday."

Andrew was circumspect. He appreciated his psychic friend's ability to articulate certain ideas for which he could not find words. "You know, I've often imagined Clare as my soul mate. Heaven sent us to earth with no memory of each other and placed us in proximity to see what would happen if we met on earth. It's a way of explaining why I felt I loved Clare even before I met her. A pretty crazy idea, I guess."

"The world doesn't teach us to think that way. The world teaches that money, possessions, and good grades define us. Yet, the prestige we get from the house we live in and the car we drive is meaningless compared to the love we give and the love we receive. No, it's not a crazy idea. It's an interesting idea."

"I agree, but love is a two-way street, right? I used to wonder if loving Clare without her loving me back meant that my love for her wasn't genuine love. I've always known I was only kidding myself about that point. No matter how I turned it over in my heart, mind, and soul, I've always known my love for Clare is my great truth." He paused for a moment before saying, "It hurts too much not to be real."

"Love isn't always a joint experience. Sometimes the beloved doesn't reciprocate, and that's a hard idea for a loving heart to accept. I've worked with people in that circumstance, but that's not what's going on here."

"What do you mean?"

Robin tucked a strand of her black hair behind her ear. "Psychically, I sense you are not in love alone."

8

AUTUMN HAZE PARK

The mist dissipated, and Clare found herself outside of Room 20 in the Intensive Care Unit of Bay Memorial Hospital. It took her a moment to realize she had jumped from Andrew's house in the Florida Keys to the hospital. Gathering her bearings, she couldn't help but wonder what strange force was moving her from place to place, and for what purpose?

Clare glanced around for her spirit guide, but there was no sign of him. She entered the nondescript hospital room with its plain cream-colored walls and observed her comatose physical body connected to monitors, intravenous drips, and mechanical ventilation. According to her basic understanding, a comatose person does not respond to pain, touch, or light. Her body was oddly inert and deeply asleep.

The door opened and Sam entered, carrying a single rose in a plastic vase and a picture in a frame. He placed the items on the table next to the bed. The photo was a keepsake from a day in late October 1972. Clare and Andrew had taken the ninety-minute drive from Millville College to hike in Autumn Haze State Park. On that chilly fall morning, they hiked the trail to one of the park's two lakes. Walking on a bed of fallen leaves a few steps ahead of Andrew, Clare heard him call her name. She innocently turned around, and Andrew snapped the picture. Clare often took the picture out and fondly remembered the beauty of that day. She never told Sam the story behind the picture. He only knew she liked it.

It startled Clare when she heard a voice coming from behind her. "Sam's been told to prepare for the worst." Jerome Emiliani was now standing with her.

"I guess that means I'm going to die," Clare said in a tone of resignation.

"That's not important right now. Let's take a walk. I have something to show you."

Clare wondered what could be more important than whether she would live or die. Deciding she had little choice, she followed her spirit guide out of the room, through the common area of the Intensive Care Unit, and into the hallway. They left the hospital and entered the spirit realm, an outdoor wooded area under a brilliant blue sky. A chorus of birdsong resonated from the trees overhead. At the edge of the adjacent lake, the carp made little splashing sounds among the water lilies.

"How does this happen?" Clare asked. "How do I hop from one place to another?"

Jerome offered only a knowing smile in response.

"Where are we? Is this heaven?"

Jerome waved his arm in a sweeping motion. "Take another look around."

"This is Autumn Haze Park! How did you know about this place? And why are we here?"

"For his release," Jerome said.

"What do you mean?" Clare stepped toward the lake and realized her guide had vanished. Emiliani's sudden appearances and departures no longer surprised her, but his vague answers and veiled references still frustrated her.

Walking alone, she wandered around the edge of the lake and viewed the sunlight dancing across the water, which made the scene even more picturesque. Almost immediately, Clare entered a clearing where she observed a young man sitting on a wooden bench. When he saw her, he stood as if he'd been waiting for her. She noted he wore his hair in a pompadour style; he dressed in a black leather jacket with a turned-up collar, jeans, and black boots.

What struck her most about this fellow was his youth. He couldn't have been much older than the students she'd taught at St. Ann High School.

He uttered her name. "Clare?"

Because this person was a stranger, she hesitated. "Yes, do I know you?"

"I'm Paul McGovern, your father, your biological father."

"But you are way too young to be my father, and if you *are* my father, what are you doing here?"

"During my earthly life, I never knew I had a child. If I had known, maybe I would have lived a different lifestyle."

"Are you telling me you're dead?"

"We don't call it death, but yeah, I've passed from physical existence, and I'm here now to explain a few things and to hear about your life."

"Oh?"

"Your mother and I were teenagers, too young to have a baby."

"Hold on. Who's my mother? Is she here too?"

"No, she's still in the physical world. Her name is Doreen Norton. She has a husband now and is doing all right, but she had a rough childhood. Anyway, I was known as Kid Switchblade, and I was part of a gang that stole cars for parts. One night, we were out on the street and ran into a rival gang. We got into it, and two members of the other gang did me."

Clare was almost too afraid to ask. "What do you mean by *did you*?"

"They shoved me in a dark alleyway and beat me up. They finished me by slitting my throat. Once they shoved me in the alley, I knew I was in for a beating, but I figured they'd just bloody me up and let me go. Instead, one of them found a switchblade in my jacket pocket and thought it'd be ironic if he used it on me."

"Two rival gang members murdered you?"

Paul nodded. "Yeah, imagine that: the infamous Kid Switchblade getting killed by his own knife. Believe me, Clare. If I'd known about you, I would have wanted to be involved in your life. I'm not sure how that would have worked out under the circumstances, but that's what I would have wanted."

"Why were you even in a gang?"

"The gang was my family. I didn't have anybody else."

"How did you live? I mean, what did you do for money?"

Paul grinned sheepishly. "Stealing cars, mostly, and we did whatever else we had to do to survive. I'm not saying it was right, but we did what we had to do."

Clare said nothing for a few minutes. Throughout her life, she had wondered about her parents and why they had given her up. Now, hearing Paul McGovern's story, she understood why her life had taken such an unstable path in the foster care system of the 1950s and 1960s. Even though Paul's life had been short and his death had been violent, meeting her father in the spirit realm gave her a sense of peace.

"Will you tell me about your life, Clare?"

"Until now, I didn't understand how I'd gotten into the foster care system, but as well as I can remember, I went through a series of at least twenty foster homes. I never felt as if I belonged any-where. I was in one placement after another, but I made the best of it. When I was fourteen, I was with the Stevenson family, and a so-cial worker told me I was too old and nobody would adopt me. The social worker said I'd have to quit school and go to work in a cou-ple of years. I remember crying so hard and so long when I heard that. I told Sarah Sperling, my best friend at school, and she told her mother. Sarah's mom took me in and treated me like her own daughter, even though she had three girls of her own and Sarah's father was deceased. That stability helped me to excel academically in high school and college. I married my high school sweetheart, but we're divorcing. Now I'm living with a restaurant owner."

"I'm sorry you had to move around so much," Paul said. "Hearing that only makes me wish I could have been there for you. At least Sarah's mom got you settled, and that helped you pull your life to-gether. She sounds like a saint of a woman."

Clare agreed.

"What about this restaurant owner?" Paul asked. "Is he a good guy?"

"Good enough, I guess."

"Sounds like you have doubts."

"Sam can be a little demanding, and he's unpleasant when he drinks too much, but he owns a successful restaurant. We're doing okay."

"Maybe you should be wary of him. It sounds like you are getting some warning signs."

Clare laughed. "Wow, you really do sound like my father. You're counseling me about my boyfriend."

Paul looked into the sky at a flock of birds flying overhead and uttered, "Uh-oh!"

"What is it?"

"Those birds are my cue."

"What cue?"

"My cue to say goodbye."

Clare protested. "Don't go! I have about a thousand more questions to ask you."

As Paul's image faded, his voice echoed, "Saint Jerome will take care of you."

"*Saint* Jerome?"

With Paul gone and Jerome nowhere around, Clare was alone on the shore of the oval-shaped lake, contemplating the connection she just made with the father she'd never known. Perhaps she had judged her father too harshly for not being in her life. She had rejected him because she assumed he had rejected her. In the physical world, her dad knew nothing about Clare. Clare's mother, Doreen, gave up her baby, hoping that someone would offer the child a better life than she could provide. Her parents were good people with the best of intent.

Jerome emerged in the clearing. "Souls carry the wounds of childhood into adulthood," he said. "You are here today to take on a spiritual task, which is to understand your biological parents. Souls must forgive the past and the present before they can find their path to the future."

It was Clare's moment of reconciliation; she no longer blamed her parents for her tough childhood. She now had a better understanding of her parents' situation at the time of her birth. Without this insight, she would never have been able to forgive them.

"Jerome, I am no longer judgmental. Whatever mistakes my parents made, I feel no sense of condemnation."

Emiliani smiled. "I have to leave you again, but you still have spiritual work to do."

"Wait! Where are you going?" But she got no answer before her spirit guide dematerialized.

9

SAM'S REPORT

At exactly eleven o'clock, Andrew called South Amboy Marina Café from his kitchen phone. He didn't want to let on that he knew about Clare's coma, nor did he want to say he'd been in contact with Clare's spirit for fear the person on the other end of the phone would think he was some crackpot and hang up.

The female who answered the telephone sounded very young and identified herself as Lydia. "Hello, my name is Andrew, and I'm an old friend of Clare's. I wonder if I might speak to Clare if she's available."

"Oh," Lydia said. "No, Clare's not here right now. Would you like to leave a message?"

Lydia's response did not surprise Andrew. She possibly didn't know much, or perhaps Sam had instructed his staff to refer such calls to him. "What about Sam? Is he available?"

"Let me check. Hold on, please."

"Thanks, I'll hold." He nodded to Robin to signal he thought he was making progress.

A male voice answered the phone. "This is Sam. To whom am I speaking?"

Andrew maintained a cordial tone. "Thanks for taking my call, Sam. My name's Andrew Leahy. I'm an old friend of Clare's. We were in school together at Millville College, and I'd like to see her. I understand she works at the restaurant. Can I leave a message?"

Sam paused before he spoke again. "Clare isn't well enough to entertain visitors."

"Sorry to hear that. It sounds serious."

Sam's voice became subdued. "It is serious, Mr. Leahy, and we need some privacy. So, if you'll excuse me..."

Andrew tried to keep Sam on the line a moment longer. "I can respect your desire for privacy, and I don't mean to bother you if this is a difficult time, but Clare and I were close friends in college. I regret we haven't stayed in touch over the years." He hesitated before uttering the next sentence. "You make it sound like a life-threatening situation."

"I'm afraid it is. Frankly, Mr. Leahy, I'm sorry to say it may come down to removing Clare from life support and letting her go."

"No, I'm so sorry to hear that. I don't know what to say."

"We have made no decision, but it doesn't look like Clare's going to make it."

"Again, I'm so, so sorry."

"If you'll excuse me, I've got a restaurant to run."

"One more thing, please," Andrew said. "What hospital is Clare in?"

"Bay Memorial, but you wouldn't be able to visit her, if that's what you're thinking."

"I understand. Thank you for your time, Sam. I'll keep Clare in my prayers."

"Thank you."

Andrew hung up the telephone. "Robin, I'm going to South Amboy. Will you come with me?"

"Don't you have a show coming up next weekend?" she asked. "Will you be back in time?"

"Yeah, you're right, and we have rehearsals during the week, but I can't let the doctors pull the plug on Clare!"

"What will you do there?"

Andrew shook his head. "No idea. Maybe I can convince Sam or the doctors that Clare wants to live."

"No one will listen to you."

"Or I will tell Sam that Clare's spirit visited me in Florida while she was in a coma, and they shouldn't end her life until we understand what this spirit stuff is all about. He'll have to listen to me."

"Good luck with that!" Robin snickered. "I meet skeptics, cynics, and nonbelievers all the time. If Sam falls into one or more of those categories, he may just stop talking to you completely. Be careful not to alienate him."

"I understand what you mean, but I can't think of any other way."

"Maybe you should prepare yourself for the possibility that Clare may leave the physical world once they remove life support."

Andrew sighed. "Maybe that's inevitable, but I cannot imagine a world without Clare. If that's the case, why did she appear here in spirit this morning? I must tell her I love her one more time."

"It's possible," Robin offered, "that Clare's spirit came here because the Universe was giving you that chance. Perhaps her spirit needs to know that before vacating the earthly plane. The other possibility is that the Universe is giving you another chance to tell her you love her to make some peace with it. Of course, it could be a combination of both things."

Andrew insisted he had to make the trip to South Amboy. "I don't have a plan, but even if it doesn't turn out well, I've got to try."

"When are you leaving?"

Andrew retrieved his address book to look for the airline number. "I can leave tomorrow. There used to be a late afternoon flight back home. I can stay in my old house with Uncle Ed." Before calling for the reservation, he again appealed to Robin. "I need my psychic sidekick."

"It might help me to get away from the press and all the hoopla," Robin said. "I need to get out of the public eye and make the media forget about me."

"And if that doesn't work, maybe you can cast a spell, so the media fixates on the new single by the Overseas Highwaymen."

"Oh, that's real funny! That's the mentality that got me into this situation."

"Come on! I'm just kidding."

"Okay, okay, I'll go. What's next?"

"Why don't you go home and pack? Meanwhile, I'll book us a flight and call you about the details."

"What about your commitments here?"

Andrew chuckled. "The band is at a tenuous point. We haven't yet signed any contracts, and I'm afraid of what will happen in terms of negotiations if the front man walks out on a couple of gigs."

"Andrew, you've got a number one record nationally, and another record is getting radio play. No one is going to throw you to the curb."

"Is that your professional psychic prediction?"

Robin made a face. "Big stars cancel appearances all the time. Just say you're going to South Amboy for a personal matter."

"Let's not give away our destination. Otherwise, we'll take the media circus with us."

Robin didn't think of that. "I'd hate to imagine the headline if the media knew the actual reason we're going to South Amboy: *Leahy Abandons Summer Tour to Chase Ghost of Lost Love.* How weird would that be?"

"When you put it that way, it sounds weird, but that doesn't mean it's far from the truth."

10

UNDER THE COVERS

Alone on the shore of the lake, Clare wondered what Jerome Emiliani meant when he said she had more spiritual work to do. Did he mean she should sit by the water and meditate or pray? Would her father reappear for additional discussion? Or would another spirit mysteriously emerge from the bushes? She didn't know.

Her spirit shifted to the front door of the house she shared with Sam. It was nighttime, and the lights were off, which made her think Sam hadn't gotten home yet, or maybe he was sitting with her body at the hospital. The locked front door was no barrier because her spirit took on a translucent state, which allowed her to pass through the solid entrance. Even in the dark, her eyes could see. The clock on the wall showed it was after one o'clock in the morning, so she assumed Sam must be sound asleep upstairs. From the foot of the staircase, she heard the toilet flush.

"Sam, I'm home!" Hearing no response, she ascended the stairs. "Sam, it's me, Clare," she shouted louder, but still no reply. Clare passed through the bedroom door just as she had passed through the front door. What she saw next utterly shocked her.

Sam was standing next to the bed wearing only a white T-shirt and no bottoms. An opened bottle of vodka and two empty glasses sat on the night table. Someone had strewn a South Amboy Marina Café uniform and a pair of women's panties across the floor. Clare knew immediately that the uniform wasn't hers by the name tag—*Lydia*. Her eyes detected some slight movement under the bedcovers.

"I know you're in there," Sam said flirtatiously. "Come on now, Lydia. Let me see."

Lydia revealed herself by pulling the sheet and blanket from over her head. She enticed Sam to get on top of her. As Sam tried to kiss her, she said, "No, not yet!" They both giggled as Lydia teasingly pulled off Sam's undershirt. "Okay," she said with feigned prudishness. "You may kiss me now."

Angered, Clare wondered what Sam thought he was doing with an eighteen-year-old girl in their bed.

Unlike the time she'd learned about Jason and Janine, Clare didn't yell and scream. She wouldn't have done so even if Sam could hear her. She felt hurt more by Jason's affair because Janine had been a trusted friend. Lydia was young enough to be Sam's daughter. As for Sam, she thought, *He's so not worth it!*

Clare left Sam and Lydia in the bedroom. She made her way to the kitchen, where she found Jerome sitting at the table in Sam's usual chair, enjoying a cup of coffee. "Take a memo! If Clare survives, she's breaking it off with Sam."

Emiliani stood up for Clare as he'd done in the restaurant. "I hope you don't mind, but I've made a pot of coffee. May I pour some for you?"

"Since when do spirits drink coffee?"

"Oh, do you prefer a tea? I believe I saw some herbal tea in your cabinet."

"I'll stick to coffee. I drink it black."

"Of course," Jerome said, reaching for the coffeepot.

Clare took her first sip. "I guess you know Sam is upstairs screwing an eighteen-year-old girl."

"No, Clare. That's not accurate."

"What do you mean? I was just up there. He's with Lydia from the restaurant. They are both naked in my bed. I left before the main event, but I know what's going on."

Jerome reached for a napkin and wiped a spot of coffee from his beard. "I understand you may be a little *edgy*, but Lydia isn't eighteen."

"She's not?"

"She's sixteen. Lydia lied about her age when she applied for the job at the restaurant because she thought Sam wouldn't have hired her as a sixteen-year-old."

"How do you know that?"

"I get information on a need-to-know basis."

Clare rubbed her temples and growled. "Sam is upstairs having sex with a minor and plying her with alcohol—all while I'm in a coma."

"I'm sorry," Emiliani said, "but at least the coffee can't get you more agitated."

"Don't be so sure of that!"

"No, what I mean is caffeine is a central nervous system stimulant, but since you're not with your body, the caffeine won't keep you up at night."

"My central nervous system is out of commission with a deadly form of bacterial meningitis. I'll have a second cup!"

Jerome poured more coffee. "I wonder if I might trouble you for a few of those miniature chocolate chip cookies. There's a box hidden behind a sauce jar."

"That's Sam's secret stash. He thinks I don't know about it, but I do." Clare retrieved the box. "So, you like chocolate chip cookies?"

"I do. Thank you!"

"When we were at the lake, you said I had spiritual work to do. Well, my spiritual work leads me to conclude all men are bad, and if I get out of this coma, I'm going to avoid relationships with men forever."

Jerome shook his head. "The point of this experience is not to obstruct your practice of love. Nor is it to reinforce the hardness you've learned over your earthly existence. If you remember our conversation in the restaurant, I said you were going to have a transformative experience."

"I remember."

"The purpose of a relationship can be to challenge a person's values, attitudes, and beliefs. Love is spiritual rather than material. Love requires you to burrow through a hole in the wall that is blocking your heart. That is the transformative experience of which I spoke."

Clare struggled to apply Jerome Emiliani's words to her own life. "Are you saying my heart is too hard, too hard to love another person?"

"Do not put the material aspects of life before the spiritual aspects of love."

After giving some thought to Jerome's words, she was ready to argue. "The world is a material place. A person can't live off love alone. People have to pay for things."

"True, but a person can't base everything on money, possessions, or security."

Clare slid the package of cookies across the table. "You seem to enjoy worldly pleasures. Would you like another?"

"Thank you," Emiliani said without hesitation. "Why did you marry Jason, and why are you with Sam?"

Clare raised her eyebrows. "Excuse me!"

"You think I'm being audacious, don't you?"

"Ordinarily I would, but under the circumstances, let me answer the question. I needed someone to give my life stability. As a child, they passed me from one home to another like a hot potato. I need to feel as though I belong, to know I'll be in one place with one person without having to worry about being plucked up and moved to the next living arrangement. Is there anything wrong with that?"

"In the world of form, physical and economic needs are practical considerations. Yet, a truly enlightened individual does not follow a materialistically driven worldview. She sees the spiritual side of love and has faith other things will follow according to *plan*."

Jerome paused to let Clare absorb this awareness before he continued, "It never ceases to amaze me how people either mistake something else for love, or they don't recognize love once it appears. I am bewildered when someone prays for that one great love, only to ignore or deny it once it arrives."

"Maybe the person praying for love gets surprised when it comes. She is frightened by its power and prefers the comfortable life she's mapped out."

Clare had dated Jason as a young teenager and charted a course whereby he would be her protector and provider. When that plan failed, Sam offered her another chance at the permanence she so craved. Now, it was clear. Sam had betrayed her as well, and the likelihood she could work this out with him was zilch. "I sort of get it," Clare said, "but it seems you think romance is like a fairy tale, and fairy tales are for kids. Fairy tales aren't true."

Emiliani smiled in that paternalistic way of his. "When love is true, it is not a fairy tale. It is not make-believe. The world will pass, but love will not. Love endures. Love is eternal."

"Is it true of other types of love?"

He reached for another cookie. "It is helpful for people's understanding to put love into different categories. Romantic love or sexual love is one kind. We love our families and friends. We show love and goodwill toward humanity. These are some ways people distinguish one kind of love from another. Yet, spiritually there are no categories of love; all love comes from the same *source*. The answer to your question is yes. All true love is everlasting."

"You seem to *love* chocolate chip cookies," Clare said teasingly.

"Indeed!" Emiliani said. "Another way to use the word *love*."

"What happens next?"

"What do you want to happen?"

"Well, I'd like to wake up from this coma."

"I'm afraid that's not my call. Is there anything else?"

"I met my biological father at the lake. He told me my mother's name is Doreen Norton, and she is alive in the physical world. I want to meet her, but if I do, will she be able to see me? Will I be able to talk with her?"

Jerome leaned back in his chair and tugged on his beard. "No, she won't. You will need someone in the physical world to intercede. It would have to be someone who can see you and speak to you, but I don't suppose you know anyone like that, do you?"

11

SOUTH AMBOY ARRIVAL

LATE NIGHT, MAY 8, 1985

C atching one of the last flights out of Key West, Andrew and Robin had to change planes in Atlanta before continuing to their destination.

Andrew arranged for them to be picked up by his uncle Ed, who would serve as their host in South Amboy. Upon landing, Andrew and Robin deplaned and retrieved their luggage. They took the escalator down to the baggage claim area where Ed Leahy waited for them.

"There's my uncle." Andrew pointed to a man of about sixty, with a full head of thick white hair, near the baggage carousel.

Ed Leahy met them at the bottom of the escalator and offered a hardy handshake to Andrew. "You must be Andrew's friend," he said to Robin.

"I'm Robin Karoly. Thanks for coming out on such short notice to pick us up."

"Call me Ed or Uncle Ed. I hope I have time to get to know you while you're here, Robin, but first, let's get your bags."

Robin chatted with Andrew's uncle on the way from the terminal to the parking lot. "Are you as musically inclined as your nephew?"

"Not at all," Ed said. "He gets that from his mother's side of the family. Let's say I'm more mechanically inclined. I just finished re-storing a 1949 Chevrolet Deluxe 350 V8. It's in the garage out back. If you're interested, I'll show it to you."

"Uncle Ed, you've had that old car out back since before I left home."

"It takes time and money. My baby still needs some minor work, but she's registered and ready for the road. Wait until you see the killer custom paint job on her. She's a beauty! You can use her while you're here, Andrew, as long as you can handle the three-speed manual transmission on the column."

"Don't you remember, Uncle Ed? I took my driving test with a three-on-the-column. It'll be cool driving that old Chevy. Thanks."

"I don't drive it often, but when I do, the car turns heads."

"What do you do for work, Ed?" Robin asked, changing the topic.

"I'm service manager at a Chevy dealership."

"Oh, that makes sense," Robin said. "You must know a lot about cars."

"Yes, I do." Uncle Ed unlocked the trunk of his new Impala in the airport parking lot. "I've only had this car for a few months."

As they reached the outskirts of South Amboy, Uncle Ed asked Andrew about the purpose of his visit. "You sounded so rushed on the phone, and you never told me why you were coming home. Of course, you are welcome anytime, but what's going on? I thought you were so busy with your music."

Andrew never intended to explain the reason for his trip home to Uncle Ed, and he had no intention of telling his uncle that Robin was a psychic. "Oh, I just needed a break, so please don't tell anyone we're staying with you."

"Why? You're my nephew, Andrew, and I'm proud of you. I've already told some folks you'll be staying with me."

Andrew grumbled, "If people know I'm here, it will cause a media circus. Believe me."

Uncle Ed laughed. "You make it sound like you and Robin are on some secret mission instead of having a little getaway."

It was going on one forty-five in the morning by the time Uncle Ed turned his Chevy Impala onto North Point Road. For Andrew, returning to the home of his youth made the complexities of being a rock star evaporate. The porch light was on, and its yellow glow emitted a signal of welcome. Andrew half expected to see his mother open the front door and greet them.

Once inside the foyer, Uncle Ed said, "You and Robin can have the master bedroom." He carried the larger of Robin's two suitcases upstairs.

Robin smiled at Andrew. "He thinks we're a couple. Are we sleeping in the same room?"

Andrew chuckled. "I didn't explain to Uncle Ed why I was coming home or who you are or why you came with me. If he knows you're a psychic, it'll lead to many questions. I'll sleep on the couch tonight and make some explanation in the morning."

Uncle Ed called to Robin from the top step. "I'll let Andrew carry your other bag upstairs. I've got to get up in about three hours for work, so I need to sleep."

"Good night," Robin said. "Thanks for picking us up, Mr. Leahy, and thanks for the hospitality. Andrew will get my other bag."

"I'm happy to have you here. Oh, and again please call me Ed."

Robin waved. "Good night, Ed."

Andrew gestured to Robin. "Come on, I'll show you to your room. Tomorrow I'll explain to my uncle that we're not a couple. No big deal."

Robin yawned. "I'm tired. I just want to lay my head on a pillow and close my eyes."

Andrew retrieved a blanket from the hallway linen closet for her before turning off the light.

Downstairs, he made a bed on the couch and fell asleep right away until a knock on the door interrupted his rest. At first, he thought he was dreaming, but a second knock was more insistent. He doubted Uncle Ed expected any visitors, and North Point Road was a dead-end street with virtually no overnight traffic. He peered out from behind the curtains of the bay window to see a woman.

Andrew opened the front door and said nothing at first. He simply put his arm around Clare's shoulder, savoring the heaven-sent warmth of her body against his.

Clare quipped, "I keep showing up on your doorstep."

"Yes, you do, and I'd never turn you away. How did you find me here?"

She rolled her eyes. "Oh, you know. One minute I was philosophizing with Jerome Emiliani at my kitchen table. The next I was standing on the front porch of your parents' house. I figured I should knock."

"My uncle Ed lives here now. He picked us up at the airport tonight, but he and Robin are sleeping in the two bedrooms on the second floor. I'm taking the couch for tonight."

"Oh, Robin is here too?"

"Yeah, I brought Robin with me. I thought her psychic abilities might come in handy. We came here to find your physical body, which we know is at Bay Memorial Hospital. Beyond that, I don't have a viable plan."

"How did you know the hospital name?"

"I called South Amboy Marina Café for any information about you. Sam told me you were critically ill at the Bay Memorial on life support."

"So, you spoke to Sam?"

"I did. He sounded like a decent guy."

"Oh, you think Sam sounds decent, do you?" Clare sighed. "Where do I begin?"

"Let me move the linens and pillow so we can sit on the couch. Since Uncle Ed and Robin are asleep upstairs, I guess they can't hear your voice, and I'll try not to talk too loudly."

Clare laughed. "I guess you'd look kind of funny if someone came downstairs and found you in a one-way conversation."

"I guess so. Why don't you start with what happened after you left my Florida house?"

"I have something to tell you about Sam. First, I want to tell you about Autumn Haze State Park."

"Do you mean the park where we hiked around the lake?"

"Yep, only this park wasn't in the physical world. I think it was the spirit realm's version of Autumn Haze Park. Jerome dropped me off there, and I met the spirit of my biological father—Kid Switchblade—by that same lake."

"I'm not sure I follow you. You met your father, your biological father, and his name is *Kid Switchblade*?"

"Maybe I should slow down," Clare said, stopping to take a breath. "My father's real name is Paul McGovern. In the early 1950s, he was in a gang stealing cars. After he got my mom pregnant, a rival gang pushed him into an alleyway and slit his throat. He died not knowing my mom was pregnant with me."

"What a story!"

"Isn't it great?"

Andrew frowned. "I wouldn't call it great. After all, someone died."

"No, I don't mean my father's murder is great. I mean, it's great I know my father, and I know why I didn't have an actual family growing up. My parents were teenagers. They were too young to care for me. Going through the foster care system was hard, but growing up in a gang environment would have been difficult too."

"I guess that must give you some sort of resolution."

"Yes and the other good thing is I know my mother's name. It's Doreen Norton, and she is alive in the physical world." Clare became serious. "I have to tell you what happened since I last saw you."

"What's that?"

"After I met my father at the lake, my spirit moved to the house that I share with Sam." Clare hesitated for a moment. "It was night-time, so I went upstairs to look for him, hoping I could somehow communicate with him."

"Was he there?"

"Oh, he was in the bedroom, but he wasn't alone. A girl was with him. Her name is Lydia."

Andrew remembered Lydia from the phone call to the restaurant.

"Lydia is only sixteen years old. Sam was in our bed with her."

"Oh?"

Clare's lips tightened. "Jason cheated on me with my friend, but this is far worse because Lydia is a minor."

"Were they aware of your presence?"

"No, and I was standing right next to the bed. I left before they had sex." She punctuated the word *sex*.

"You understand Sam has committed a serious crime, don't you?" Andrew asked. "I'm sure the authorities would be interested. Lydia is a victim."

Throughout the night, Andrew and Clare brainstormed about how to stop the hospital from taking her off life support. At one point, Andrew suggested he should tell Sam that Clare's spirit appeared and said she wants to live.

"No! Don't do that, especially if Sam's been drinking. He'll think you're some kind of nut, and he has no patience for people with unconventional ideas. You'll have to convince him you're my friend and you have my best interest at heart. Act as if you're on his side."

In the morning, Uncle Ed came downstairs and heard Andrew's voice. "I didn't know you talk in your sleep. You sounded as if you were talking to the devil himself for practically the entire night."

Andrew explained the noise by saying he'd been watching television. "Sorry if I disturbed you."

"Did you have a fight with your lady or something?"

"Uncle Ed, you misunderstand the nature of my relationship with Robin. We're not a couple. We're just traveling together. I won't be sharing a room with her while we're here."

Ed scratched his head as he turned on the coffee maker. "Why didn't you mention it last night?"

"I don't know. It was getting late and..."

"Never mind, I figured you were a rock star and the ladies were all over you. Tell me, do you have a girlfriend?"

Andrew noted Clare's enjoyment at the way this conversation was unfolding. "No one to speak of."

Uncle Ed chuckled. "Does that mean there's someone, but you just can't tell me about her, or there's no one, period?"

Clare stifled a grin. "Tell him you were up with the ghost of your long-lost love."

Andrew knew Clare had meant her comment as a joke, but her attempt at humor contained more truth than she realized.

When Andrew didn't answer, Uncle Ed regarded him with squinted eyes. He placed the piping hot cup in front of Andrew. "Do you still take it with milk?"

"Yes."

Still amused, Clare said, "Be careful when you're talking to me and there is someone else around, Andrew. Someone may think you're out of your mind."

"I don't care. I've got something important to say to you."

Ed believed Andrew was addressing him. "If you've got something on your mind, let's hear it."

"Sorry, Uncle Ed," Andrew said. "I wasn't talking to you. I was just working out some new lyrics."

Uncle Ed placed the car keys to the '49 Chevy on the table. "Are you okay? You're acting strangely this morning."

"I'm okay. It's just that I have a lot on my mind with the summer tour, contracts, writing new songs, and so forth."

"Well, if you'll excuse me," Uncle Ed said, "I have to head out. I'm opening today, and I have to be on time."

No sooner had Uncle Ed left than Robin descended the staircase, stopping on the last step. "Clare's spirit has been here. Did you know that?"

"She knocked on the door last night the way she did at my Florida house," Andrew said. "Clare's been here all night. Are you able to sense her presence psychically?"

"Not directly, but I can sense changes in you, Andrew. You give off a distinct vibration when you are near Clare."

Andrew considered that concept. "Do I?"

"Excuse me, Andrew," Clare said, as that peculiar vapor enveloped her again. "I think I'm leaving now, but I have to ask you a favor. Find my mother, Doreen Norton!"

12

VALENTINE'S DAY LOVE LETTER

Thursday, May 9, 1985

"Clare's gone again," Andrew said. "She asked us to find her mother, but all she gave us is a name—a Doreen Norton."

"With no other clues, that's a tough challenge," Robin said. "We should drop by the hospital first. If Clare's spirit has returned to her body, maybe I'll be able to sense something, assuming we get in to see her."

"It's still too early for visiting hours, which gives us time for breakfast and to brainstorm how to locate Clare's mother." Andrew set out some dishes.

"I have an interesting theory about why Clare's spirit jumps around so much," Robin said.

"What is it?"

"Nothing in the Universe is random. Clare appears in one place or another for a specific purpose. When she fulfills that purpose, the Universe sends her on."

"That makes sense because as soon as she asked us to find her mother, she disappeared."

Robin agreed. "Her purpose was to seek you out to find Doreen Norton."

After a couple of hours, Andrew grabbed the keys for the '49 Chevy and led Robin to the classic vehicle in the garage. A cover made of a soft, stretchy material protected the car. Andrew removed the overlay and fixed his eyes upon a gleaming metallic-green automobile. "Wow! She's in pristine condition."

"It is impressive!"

"Everything appears to be brand new right down to the white-wall tires." He opened the passenger door for Robin. "I can't believe what my uncle has done with this, the clock, the push-button radio."

"Is the upholstery original?" Robin asked.

"No, but it's very authentic looking."

Robin opened the glove compartment. "I hope your uncle doesn't mind, but I suddenly feel drawn to look in here."

"That's a good idea," Andrew said. "Look for the insurance and registration cards. Uncle Ed said we can drive the car legally, but it doesn't hurt to be sure."

Robin removed a folded envelope yellowed with age. She carefully took out the documents. "Well, Edward Leahy of North Point Road is the registered owner, and here's the insurance card," she said, handing the paperwork to Andrew.

Andrew looked over the documents and handed them back to Robin. "Everything is in order. Let's go!"

As Robin put the documents back, she noticed something else in the envelope. She took out a folded note, which had also yellowed with age. "I knew something drew me to snoop in the glove compartment," she said, opening the paper. "It's a letter to someone named *Doreen* from someone named *Paul*, and it's dated February 14, 1952."

"Isn't that interesting? Let me see it, please." The outside of the envelope displayed a three-cent stamp with no address. Andrew opened the letter and paused for a moment. "This is beyond coincidence. This must be a letter from Clare's father to her mother."

"The Universe *meant* for us to find this," Robin said. "It's Paul's Valentine's Day letter to Doreen. Maybe he intended to include a card, but something happened, and he never got it to Doreen. Can you read it out loud?"

Andrew cleared his throat.

Dear Doreen,

I don't need Valentine's Day to remind me that I love you. I am as sure of my love for you as anyone could be about such a thing. It was Valentine's Day just one year ago today when I first saw you in Don's Luncheonette. The place was like Antsville, and you were working behind the counter making a root beer float for your friend, Cynthia, who was talking about wanting to see a new movie called *Love Is Better Than Ever* at the Majestic Theater around the corner.

That day, I never thought you'd talk to a greaser like me, but you did. I know you noticed me noticing you. "Can I help you with something?" you asked, but I was so tongue-tied I couldn't answer. I can talk tough to some punk, but I don't know what to say to a pretty girl.

Cynthia tried to move things along when she said, "Oh, Doreen, I think the poor boy is so enchanted with you he can't speak."

I finally recovered and asked for a burger. I guess you could say the rest is history.

Well, you bring out the best in me, so I have something important to tell you when we meet tonight in our usual place.

Love,
Paul

"What do you think Paul wanted to tell Doreen?" Robin asked.

"I don't know, but it must have been important to him or both of them."

"What does 'Antsville' mean?"

Andrew laughed. "Nineteen-fifties slang for very crowded. You know, customers crawling around the place like ants."

"This letter gives us some clues," Robin said. "Have you ever heard of Don's Luncheonette or the Majestic Theater?"

"No, I haven't, and I doubt Clare has either."

Robin squinted as if trying to see into the past. "Don's Luncheonette and the Majestic Theater may no longer exist, so how do we find them?"

Andrew thought for a moment. "It would help if we could narrow it down to a city or town. We don't even know what state. Without more information, this could be frustrating."

"If one or both businesses still exist, maybe the phone company can help."

Andrew turned the key in the ignition to start the smooth-sounding engine of the old Chevy. "Good idea," he said, "but we can do that later. Let's see what's going on at the hospital." He put the car in gear and backed out of the garage. Within moments, Andrew and Robin had turned left onto North Point Road and headed for the highway toward Bay Memorial Hospital.

Fifteen minutes later, Andrew pulled into the crowded parking lot of the medical facility. He had to drive around before he saw a woman walking to her car. The woman nodded to signal she was leaving, and she pointed to her car. Andrew gave a slight wave and turned on his blinker.

Walking toward the main entrance, Robin said, "Let's think this through. What will you say when someone asks if you are a relative of the patient?"

"I'm going to say I'm the patient's brother, Andrew McGovern."

"Does Clare have a brother?"

"No, but the hospital doesn't know that."

"What if they ask to see some identification, such as a driver's license?"

Andrew smirked. "Well, unfortunately, I left it in the car."

"And who am I?"

"You're my wife, Mrs. Robin McGovern."

The ruse was unnecessary because the woman at the visitor desk barely looked at Andrew and Robin when she handed them two passes. "Only two visitors at a time," she said. "No one else is there now, but please don't stay more than twenty minutes. The elevators are around the corner; ICU is on the second floor."

Andrew and Robin walked quickly, passing a small gift shop on the way to the elevators. When the elevator door closed, Andrew pressed the button for the second floor.

"So that went well, *Andrew McGovern*," Robin quipped, using the false name Andrew had created.

"If anyone asks, stick with it, *Mrs. McGovern*."

Robin got out of the elevator ahead of Andrew. "Prepare yourself just in case Clare's physical body doesn't look like it did when you saw her in spirit."

"I've thought of that."

They entered the private ICU room, and Andrew observed Clare's body connected to so many tubes and monitors. He said nothing and just touched Clare's hand.

"Are you okay?" Robin's voice was just above a whisper.

"I know Clare is seriously ill, but seeing her like this isn't easy," Andrew said. "Do you think she feels any pain?"

"I doubt it. She's in a deep coma."

"Do you think she can hear us?"

Robin shrugged. "Why don't you try talking to her?"

Andrew leaned down and whispered into Clare's ear. "Clare, Clare, can you hear me? It's Andrew." He waited for some reaction, some sign, but the patient did not stir. He bent down again and whispered in an even lower voice, "Clare, I love you," and he kissed her cheek, hoping she would respond.

Instead, the machine at Clare's bedside alarmed, and a team of nurses and doctors raced into the room.

13

SUDDEN CARDIAC ARREST

A nurse ushered Andrew and Robin out as the medical team rushed in to begin resuscitative measures. The nurse directed them to a waiting area and asked them to "sit tight."

Standing outside of the ICU, Andrew turned to his psychic companion. "Robin, what if...?"

Robin answered before Andrew could get his words out. "I believe if Clare's body passes, her spirit will leave this earthly plane and go into the light. I say that based more on my belief system than my psychic abilities."

For Andrew, Robin's answer was what he should have expected. Again, he had to remind himself of Robin's psychic expertise—a relationship psychic as opposed to someone who communicates with the dead. "Can I say goodbye to Clare?"

Robin answered honestly, "I truly don't know, but I am afraid we must prepare for the possibility of bad news."

Andrew nodded. *Bad news!* During the years since college graduation, he had maintained hope of seeing Clare again. He now wondered if this inexplicable connection was about to be broken.

Time passed slowly as Andrew and Robin riffled through magazines. Eventually, the nurse entered. "Are you related to Ms. Rinaldi?"

"Yes," Andrew said. "I'm her brother, Andrew McGovern."

"The doctor will talk to you in a few minutes."

Andrew's voice trembled. "Is she gone?"

"No, but that's all I can say. The doctor will explain."

After fifteen more minutes of waiting, a doctor joined them in the waiting room. "Good morning, I'm Dr. Siegel, Clare's neurologist."

"Andrew McGovern," he said. "I'm Clare's brother, and this is my wife, Robin."

Dr. Siegel shook hands with both of them. "How are you?" he asked almost absentmindedly. "There's an office down the hall. Would you mind following me so we can talk in private?"

"Of course," Andrew said.

Dr. Siegel led Andrew and Robin to a small conference room and motioned for them to sit at a table. "Clare came in by ambulance six days ago," the physician said. "She collapsed at work and was unconscious by the time she reached the hospital."

"Sorry to interrupt," Andrew said. "We know meningitis is life-threatening. What are Clare's chances?"

Dr. Siegel's face gave way to surprise. "Oh, I see. You've already spoken to Mr. Agnellini?"

Andrew leaned forward in his chair. "Huh?"

"I just assumed you must have spoken to Clare's partner, Sam Agnellini, about the diagnosis," Dr. Siegel said.

Andrew played along. "That's right. Sam discussed Clare's condition with us."

Dr. Siegel reviewed the test results. "Based on her neurologic exams, brain scans, and laboratory values, she has a very lethal form of bacterial meningitis. Her kidneys are shutting down, which further contributes to an unfortunate prognosis." He paused slightly before adding, "I wish I had better news, but we give Ms. Rinaldi a two-percent chance of survival and a zero-percent chance of recovery."

Andrew digested the physician's assessment before asking, "And by survival, what do you mean?"

"I mean, if she survives, she'll remain in a persistent vegetative state."

Andrew considered the doctor's words—*persistent vegetative state*—before glancing at Robin, wondering again whether the death of Clare's body would mean the end of her out-of-body experience, which might end his interaction with her spirit.

Dr. Siegel cleared his throat. "Do you know how your sister feels about prolonging life artificially?"

"Well, I'm sure she'd want everything done. I don't think she would choose to pull the plug, if that's what you mean."

"Mr. Agnellini says she's against prolonging life artificially," the doctor stated. "Perhaps you should talk to him again. He says he has had extensive conversations with her, and Clare would not want to extend her life artificially unless some hope existed."

Robin finally spoke. "Excuse me, Dr. Siegel, but I think I see where you are going with this. Establishing the patient's wishes will help you develop an end-of-life care plan."

"That's right, Mrs. McGovern," Dr. Siegel said. "Since the patient has no living will, we turn to the closest relative. It's often the spouse, but Mr. Agnellini is not the patient's husband. I hope you will discuss this with Mr. Agnellini. I believe he has the most insight as to Clare's wishes."

"Do you know Clare is going through a divorce with Jason Rinaldi?" Andrew asked. "I mean, Jason is still legally Clare's husband. Does that make a difference?"

"Yes," the doctor said, "but it would be easier if everyone agreed."

"Can we see Clare now?" Andrew asked.

"I'll check." The doctor came back moments later to say that Andrew and Robin could see Clare.

Standing at Clare's bedside, Andrew said, "Robin, I suppose you can see what an awkward position I've put myself in. I can't pretend to be Clare's brother and give them the go-ahead to pull the plug. Besides, I'm not sure I'd do that."

"What if Sam doesn't believe you're Clare's brother? Things could get messy."

"I know. I've been trying not to think of that."

14

MEETING CASSANDRA

"**H**ello, Clare!"
A split second earlier, Clare had been sitting on a couch in Andrew's childhood living room, and now she found herself back in the spirit realm's version of Autumn Haze Park where a young-sounding female voice called to her from a park bench.

Clare called back, "Hello?"

"Come sit with me," the girl said.

The girl appeared to be about fifteen years old and wore a yellow summer dress with a flower print. A heart-shaped locket adorned the girl's neck.

"Who are you?"

Instead of answering the question, the girl repeated the invitation. "Sit with me."

Clare joined her on the bench. "You know my name. I wonder if I may know yours."

The girl scrutinized Clare with eyes the color of the deep blue ocean. She smiled sweetly, as if to invoke an underlying kinship. "I'm Cassie. I'm here to help you understand why you are having this experience."

"I have so many questions."

"I may not answer every question, but I can tell you one thing you've been wondering about." She made Clare wait before saying more.

"Please go on."

Cassie's giggle was an aural hug, as if to prolong Clare's anticipation the way younger sisters tease older siblings.

"Cassie!"

"Okay, you're going to recover from the coma."

"I am?"

"Your recovery will not be physically or psychologically easy."

"How do you know that?"

"That's not important. Saint Jerome doesn't even know yet, so let's keep it just between us."

"Saint Jerome?"

Another giggle rolled out of Cassie like a wave on a long, shallow beach. "Oh, you'll see him again. You know him as Jerome Emiliani. He was the customer who ordered the shrimp scampi and the doctor in the emergency department."

"What can you tell me about Andrew? He's the only one who can see me?"

Cassie grinned. "Oh, I'm sure you've already figured that out. If you haven't, you will."

Clare didn't press the point. "Is there anything else?"

"Just one more thing," Cassie said, unfastening the locket from around her neck. "This is for you."

"I don't understand."

"Just promise me you'll wear it from now on."

Clare attempted to open the heart, but it seemed to be jammed. "It's stuck! How does it open?"

"No, no," Cassie said, gently touching Clare's hands. "It won't open until the right time. Put it on and wear it. That's all for now."

"Can you help me put it on?"

Cassie secured the locket and said, "Your life is not in alignment."

Clare felt the locket click into place. "What does that mean—not in alignment? Not in alignment with what?" She turned around and Cassie vanished. Then the mysterious fog rolled in again.

15

A BIG BREAK

Standing quietly with Robin at Clare's bedside, the gravity of the situation hit Andrew hard. "The doctor doesn't give her much of a chance."

"No, but I get a strong sense that finding her mother is something we're supposed to do."

Andrew's eyes remained fixed on Clare. "I don't want to leave her. What if something happens while we're out playing detective?"

"Andrew, this must be hard for you. You can stay here. I'll use the phone in the lobby to see if I can get any additional information about Clare's mother. We already know her name is Doreen Norton and her father's name is Paul McGovern. They met for the first time in a place called Don's Luncheonette. We also know there was a movie theater around the corner."

"It isn't much to go on."

"I know," Robin said, "but it's something."

Andrew offered Robin some coins for the phone. "I think I would like to stay here with Clare."

Robin nodded in agreement. "Okay."

After Robin left the room, Andrew pulled a chair next to Clare's hospital bed. Even though there was little chance she could hear him, Andrew leaned into Clare's ear and whispered, "I've been carrying this around with me for fifteen years. Do you remember that snowy day when I tried to tell you about my feelings? You pooh-poohed me and said I'd get over you in three weeks. Well, you were wrong. I didn't get over you in three weeks. I still haven't gotten over you."

He stopped speaking and considered the futility of having a conversation with a comatose woman. Andrew rested his head on the railing of the bed and muttered her name, "Clare."

Moments went by before he continued. "Words are so inadequate. You can't hear me anyway, but words are all I have. I love you, Clare, truly, passionately, and eternally. I love you now and forever."

While Andrew's lips were mere inches from Clare's ear, he heard an agitated voice coming from behind him. "Who the hell are you?"

A dark-haired man stood in the doorway, dressed in a long-sleeve, ivory-colored dress shirt and black slacks. He took two steps forward and one step sideways, causing him to bump into a chair. "You must be in the wrong room." He continued to navigate a few more steps toward Andrew.

Andrew stood and extended his hand. "Andrew Leahy."

The man's demeanor changed. "Oh, Andrew," he said, as if he recognized the name. "I'm Sam Agnellini. I own this place."

Andrew realized Sam was seriously drunk.

Sam squinted and recognized his surroundings. "Wait!" He laughed. "This is the hospital. I thought I was in the restaurant. I own a restaurant. Have you ever been to South Amboy Marina Café?"

"I knew it when it was under different management—your parents, right?"

"Right you are. I should get over there. Don't worry, my friend. I'm okay to drive." He reached into his shirt pocket and pulled out a business card. "Here you go—ten percent off your bill the next time you come in. Tell them Sam sent you."

Allowing Sam to drive would be irresponsible. "Excuse me, Sam. I'd be happy to give you a ride to the restaurant or anywhere you like."

Sam rubbed his eyes and walked out. Andrew followed and

called to Sam every few steps. Sam reached an elevator just as the door opened.

Andrew got on the elevator and tried to reason with Sam. "You're too drunk to drive, Sam. Let me give you a ride."

"Do I know you?"

"We just met in Clare's room."

The elevator door opened, and Sam exited without another word.

Andrew was unsure what else to do when he noticed a uniformed security guard talking to a receptionist at the hospital's main desk. Andrew approached the guard with a sense of urgency. "Excuse me."

"Can I help you?"

Andrew pointed to Sam. "See that guy wobbling over there? He's drunk, too drunk to drive, and he's headed for his car. Maybe you can convince him not to drive."

"Okay, I'll talk to him. If he's drunk, I know what to do."

Andrew watched as the guard caught up to Sam. Although the two men were beyond earshot, Andrew surmised Sam recognized the security guard's authority and complied when the guard escorted him away.

Andrew surveyed the lobby and glimpsed Robin at one of several public telephones. As he approached, Robin was intensely writing something on a scrap of paper while continuing to talk. "Let me just be sure I've got it." She then rattled off an address. "Great! And thanks so much."

Andrew waited for Robin to hang up. "Sounds like you made some progress."

Robin nodded. "I'm trying not to get too excited, but we have a lead."

"What did you find out?"

"There was a Majestic Theater and a Don's Luncheonette in Staten Island, New York, in 1952."

"Staten Island isn't far!" Andrew said excitedly.

Robin smiled and referred to her notes. "The Majestic Theater closed in the early 1970s. It became a toy store for a time, and it's now an apartment building. But listen to this: Don's Luncheonette is still there and still in business."

"Holy moly!" Andrew exclaimed. "I can hardly believe what you're telling me!"

"It gets better. The place is currently owned and operated by Alex Olsen and his younger brother, David. I spoke with Alex, who told me their father is Don Olsen, the original owner of Don's Luncheonette. Don retired about six years ago and is in a nursing home with some form of dementia."

"That's unfortunate."

"Alex, who's now fifty-five years old, says he was already working in the kitchen in 1952, and he remembers a girl named Doreen working part-time for Don. When Doreen left the job, there was a rumor that she had gotten pregnant by some 'young ruffian,' as he described the alleged father."

"Too many coincidences," Andrew said thoughtfully. "This must be the place where Clare's mother worked. Either you're a superb detective or a really good psychic."

Robin chuckled. "A little of both and some luck, I'd say."

"Do you have the address? Let's go and find out more. Maybe we will actually find Doreen."

"We'll have to wait until Monday. Don's is closed on Mondays, and Alex offered to take us to meet his father at the nursing home. Don has a better recall of the distant past, even if he can't remember what he had for breakfast."

Andrew scratched his head. "Well, this may be the big break we need. Hopefully, Monday will be one of Don's good days."

"Do you want to return to Clare's room?" Robin asked.

"Yes, but first I'd like to buy a bouquet for her. I think I saw some fresh flowers in the gift shop. Let's brighten up the room."

"Good idea!"

Andrew made the purchase, and he and Robin headed back to the elevator. On the way, he described his brief encounter with Sam Agnellini. "The guy was drunk. I'm not sure if he realized he was in

Clare's room. He was more interested in promoting his restaurant. Sam was out of it."

Once they were alone inside the elevator, she hit the button for the ICU floor. "So, Andrew, I'm guessing Sam didn't make a good impression on you. It sounds like you think Sam isn't right for Clare."

As the elevator ascended, Andrew observed Robin's tight-lipped smile. It was the facial expression that women use when they want to conceal some secret musing. "I hope I don't run into him again."

"You will," Robin predicted, "and be careful when you do."

16

NEGOTIATING WITH THE UNIVERSE

Once the fog dissipated, instead of being in the beautiful garden, Clare was back in her hospital room, standing next to her comatose physical body. She regarded her cheerless surroundings—an old TV set hanging from the ceiling, the cream-colored walls, the well-worn tile floor, and the pervasive scent of bleach. There were stands for intravenous drips and monitors, and a box of rubber gloves. Everything was functional, but patients are not robots in for an oil change. In Clare's opinion, hospital rooms should be much less depressing with paintings on the wall. *Give me some natural beauty*, she thought. *Somebody, please bring me flowers.*

At that moment, Andrew entered the room, followed closely by Robin. "I thought you might enjoy these sunflowers," he said to the physical Clare. "Sunflowers are fascinating because they always face the sun, or so people say."

Clare called to him, "Hey, did you miss me? Guess what happened!" To her chagrin, Andrew did not respond to her. Instead, he asked Robin to find a vase or something suitable for the sunflowers.

Clare became alarmed. "Andrew, Andrew, can't you hear me? Come on, Andrew! Answer me!" But raising the volume of her voice did nothing to provoke a response.

Wearing a white lab coat and dark tie, Jerome Emiliani entered the room by passing through the door instead of opening it like a mortal. "It's time to return to your body."

Clare stared at the technology that was keeping her alive, remembering what Cassie had said in the garden. "I'm going to live! That's it, isn't it? I go back in my body, wake up, and life goes on."

"Oh, I don't know about that," Emiliani said, stroking his gray beard. "The Universe's memo only says I should get you back in your body."

Clare's thoughts sputtered for a moment. "Memo?" she asked. "The Universe communicates to you with memos?"

"Sorry, I can't explain how the Universe communicates, so I used a word I knew you'd understand. One thing I know is that you have to return to your body. I'm afraid I can't tell you what comes after that."

Clare felt as if Jerome had backed her into a corner. What if Cassie had been wrong? Clare didn't want to enter the hereafter kicking and screaming.

"Jerome, I'm not ready."

Dr. Siegel entered and shook hands with Andrew and Robin.

"I'm glad I found you here, Mr. and Mrs. McGovern," the neurologist said. "I'm arranging a meeting with Clare's family and interested parties to discuss the patient's prognosis and see if we can agree on how to proceed. Would you be available Tuesday afternoon at around two o'clock?"

Feeling discouraged, Clare turned to Emiliani. "The doctor is going to tell them there's no hope, isn't he? He's going to recommend removing life support, and I'm going to die." She gave Emiliani a moment to answer, but the spirit guide said nothing. "And why is the doctor addressing Andrew and Robin as Mr. and Mrs. McGovern?"

"Andrew told the hospital staff that he's your brother so he could be near you. The doctor believes Andrew is your relative and wants him to take part in an end-of-life discussion."

"Will Sam be there?"

"I would think so," Emiliani said. "I suspect Sam is an *interested party* the good doctor is referring to."

"Does it matter what I want or has the Universe predetermined my fate?" Clare asked angrily. She waited a moment for Emiliani to answer, but when he again said nothing, she added, "That wasn't a rhetorical question!"

"Oh," Emiliani said. "What do you want?"

"I want to live!"

Emiliani raised his bushy eyebrows. "You should realize how things are. I mean, look. You're a vegetable or rather your body is in a vegetative state."

"I'm aware of that, but let me ask you something. Do you know anyone named Cassie? I think she may be a messenger like you."

"Did you meet Cassandra?"

"She called herself Cassie. It could be short for Cassandra, I guess, but who is she?"

"Oh my, this could change everything. What did Cassandra say?"

"Well, she gave me a locket, but I can't open it."

"Brilliant! Inspirational!" Emiliani exclaimed.

"What's so inspirational?"

"I mean, it was an inspirational idea for Cassandra to give you the locket at this stage of your journey. It's just that I expected nothing like this. Did she say anything else?"

"The last thing she told me was that my plans are not in line with the Universe."

"And what plans do you think Cassandra was referring to?"

Before she could answer her spirit guide, Clare turned her attention to the conversation Dr. Siegel was having with Andrew and Robin. "Clare is in a bad way, Mr. McGovern," the physician said. "All we are doing is artificially extending her life."

"I can't say what my sister would want, but I'm not ready to take her off life support. That I know."

Dr. Siegel gave a serious yet kindly nod. "I understand, but please give it some thought. Your sister is extremely critical. If she survives, she will have a poor quality of life. We can have a more in-depth conversation tomorrow."

"Thank you, Doctor," Andrew said.

Clare turned her attention back to Emiliani. "I'll make you a deal. Let me spend more time with Andrew—twenty-four hours. And then I'll jump back in my body if you insist."

"Bargaining?" Emiliani smiled wryly. "Ordinarily, I'm not at liberty to make deals, but I should throw this one into the cosmos. Perhaps I missed a memo. I'll check my inbox and get back to you."

17

GARY

E arly on Monday morning, Andrew was raring to go to Staten Island, New York, to meet with the owners of Don's Luncheonette, the place where Clare's mother had worked as a teenager. He asked Uncle Ed to use the car again.

Uncle Ed was hesitant to let Andrew take the classic '49 Chevy to Staten Island. "I know I said I'd let you use the old car while you're here, but I thought you'd need it locally. I didn't realize you'd be taking it that far."

"Don't worry about it. I can rent a car."

"You don't have to rent a car. Take the Impala," Uncle Ed said. "I want nothing to happen to the other car. I'll park the old girl in the back of the lot. I may be working late tonight and won't be home until around nine o'clock."

"Thanks, Uncle Ed. We have to make this trip."

"What's going on in Staten Island?" Uncle Ed asked.

"We're visiting someone in a nursing home. I'm doing it as a favor for a friend. The person we're visiting has dementia."

Uncle Ed nodded. "I understand, Andrew. Both of your parents were always willing to help. I guess it's true about the apple not falling far from the tree."

Uncle Ed had already gone to work when Robin came downstairs. Andrew was brushing his teeth in the first-floor half bathroom when the wall-mounted telephone rang in the kitchen. Andrew called to Robin, "Can you get that? I'll be right there." Leaving the bathroom door open, he could hear Robin when she answered the phone on the third ring.

"Leahy residence."

Andrew wiped a spot of toothpaste from the corner of his mouth and took the receiver. "Hello."

"Hey, it's me, Gary," the caller said. "How's it going there?"

When Andrew left South Florida with Robin, he did so with no explanation to the band, except to give Uncle Ed's telephone number to his bass player in case of emergency. "Well, I've had no chance to see any of my old friends yet, but my uncle is well. You should see the '49 Chevy that Uncle Ed has restored. It's a beauty."

"Sounds great!" Gary said. "I wish I could check it out. Take a couple of pictures and show me when you get back."

"I'll see what I can do."

"When will you be back?" Gary asked, getting to the purpose of his call.

Andrew hadn't been thinking about the band. "I want to reread the contract. I'm still not so sure I like it. Is anything wrong?"

"Rehearsals haven't been going well. Billy and Alan are questioning your commitment to the band. It's not Billy so much as it is Alan. What are we doing about the contract? I have to tell them something."

Andrew was blunt. "I have a friend who is in a coma, and she's dying. She grew up in foster care and never knew her biological mother. I'm trying to find her mother. Surely, the guys can understand that."

"I don't mean to be insensitive, Andrew, but why do you have to be the one to track down your friend's biological mother?"

Andrew regretted he'd said even that much to Gary. "Because she asked me to," he answered.

"Oh, I guess you mean she asked you to find her mother before she was in a coma, huh?"

Andrew couldn't say Clare asked while she was in a coma. "That's right. We were friends in college, and she once asked me to help find her mother. I promised to help, but I didn't know how. Now that Robin is here with me, and we have an actual lead, I may finally fulfill that promise."

"I forgot you were traveling with *Lady Nadia*. I guess she's the one who uncovered this lead you're talking about."

"I know you give little credence to Robin's psychic abilities, so maybe you'll be happy to know she uncovered the lead through old-fashioned detective work. I'd like to follow up on that lead, so just tell the guys I'm helping a dying friend. Try to make them understand, and say I thank them for their patience. I'll be back soon."

"Okay, as you wish, but keep in touch with me, will you?"

"Will do," Andrew said, ending the phone call.

"How's Gary?" Robin asked, grabbing a light-blue sweater from off a couch. "Did you tell him I looked into my crystal ball and predicted he'd marry a woman with six bratty kids?"

Andrew laughed. "Gary is a confirmed bachelor. You said so yourself."

"Did I say that?" Robin chuckled. "Well, things change, you know. Maybe I can use my power to conjure up a nagging wife for him."

"I think that's what he's afraid of. Come on. Let's see what we find out on Staten Island."

18

CASSIE IN THE GARDEN

Clare remained with her body as the nurses in the physical world twice changed shifts. She estimated it must have been after seven o'clock in the morning when her spirit guide, Jerome Emiliani, reappeared with some news.

"Aha! I knew I'd find you here." He smiled. "Please go back to the garden. If you can't find Cassandra, don't worry; she'll find you. Regrettably, I can't go with you."

"Wait!" Clare said, turning her gaze to her comatose body. "Did you get any updates on whether I'll live or die?" The fog enveloped her as she strained to hear Emiliani's reply echo across dimensions.

"Oh yes. Yes, I did."

The fog thickened, and Clare was no longer in the hospital room. She was back in the garden, where Clare's physical senses felt enhanced. A crisp jasmine-scented breeze ruffled the white and magenta lily pads floating on a nearby pond. The sweet soprano of birdsong was like an auditory announcement of her return to the garden.

The same bench appeared brighter, as if sporting a fresh coat of green paint. As Clare approached the bench, she expected to see Cassie. She felt a twinge of disappointment when she saw no one there. When she sat down, most of the birds flew off, leaving the garden silent. However, not every bird abandoned Clare. A lone robin landed on the green grass directly in front of her, maybe ten feet away. Impeccably dressed in red plumage, the bird hopped toward her on black legs.

Clare addressed the feathered creature. "Well, it looks like all of your friends have flown away." The bird pecked at beetles and worms in response.

From behind her, Clare recognized Cassie's voice saying, "Who's your friend?"

Clare grinned, happy to see Cassie again. "You should have arrived a few minutes ago. Birds of every size and color occupied the garden, and they were twittering up a storm."

"I know," Cassie said. "They told me you were here." She nodded toward the robin and added, "This fellow stayed to keep you company in the meantime."

Clare regarded the bird. "I appreciate that."

Cassie cupped her hand to her mouth and chuckled. "He's been hanging around the window of the hospital room."

Clare turned sideways and faced Cassie. "Has he? And why is that?"

"He's a sort of liaison between worlds."

Clare didn't understand. "What do you mean by *liaison*?"

"He reports to me," Cassie said. "He lets me know how you're doing, or rather, how your physical body is doing while your spirit is out and about, so to speak."

"In that case, you must know my body isn't doing very well. The doctor wants to discuss taking my body off life support. I know you said I was going to live, but I feel certain the doctor wants to pull the plug."

"Trust me, dear sister! I have it on good authority the Universe intends to restore your body to health. You will continue your life in the world of form. As I say, it won't be an easy recovery, but you will emerge from the coma and return to health."

Clare liked how Cassie had addressed her—*dear sister*—because she felt a kinship with her. "That's good news," she said, still watching the robin peck at the ground before returning her gaze to the genial young girl. "Is your role to tell me I am going to live?"

"Partly, it is, but I'm also here to prepare you to return to the physical realm."

"In what way?"

"In a spiritual way," Cassie said, her eyes coming alive. "Hold on. I want to show you something."

Then the robin flew in a circle three times, and a holographic scene appeared. The visual details reminded Clare of an old movie from the silent film era because the grayish moving images had no sound. The character in the scene was a distraught teenage girl. *Letting you go shatters my heart.* When the hologram collapsed and disappeared, Clare was shaking as if she'd experienced the girl's feelings as her own. "I don't understand," she said. "What was that about?"

"That was your biological mother after she had given birth to you."

Clare took a deep breath, finally composing herself. "I felt her emotions, so distressed with a sense of loss." Then it dawned on Clare. "That happened right after she put me into foster care, didn't it?"

"That's right."

"I grew up believing my mother didn't want me, but she did, and it hurt to give me up." Clare thought about that for a moment. "I understand now."

A familiar voice came from behind. "That's what I tried to tell you. Maybe I didn't make it clear enough. When your mother gave you up, she had your best interest at heart."

When Clare turned around, she saw that the voice belonged to Paul McGovern, still wearing that pompadour hairstyle she remembered. "I know that now. I mean, I know it in my heart, not just my head." Clare stood up and walked toward her father, but he vanished before she reached him.

"There will be time to know him, but other experiences are waiting for you," Cassie said.

The robin made three more circles, and another grainy hologram appeared. This image showed Andrew continuously using a clamshell to write Clare's name in the sand at the beach, but each time he did so, a wave would wipe the inscription away. Then the hologram shrank and disappeared.

Without a word, Cassie giggled teasingly.

"What does it mean?"

Cassie rolled her eyes at Clare. "Oh, come on! Andrew is so in love with you!"

"Did that happen?" Clare asked.

"Yes, it did, and I hope you grasp the symbolism. I mean, it couldn't be any clearer."

Clare didn't answer, but the image of the waves repeatedly erasing her name stayed with her. A sense of frustration welled up inside—not her frustration but the frustration Andrew felt each time a wave rubbed out her name.

Finally, she turned to Cassie. "Ever since college graduation, I've had this vague sense Andrew was thinking about me. I can't explain it, but I felt it."

Cassie smiled subtly. "And once Andrew tried to tell you he loved you, didn't he?"

"How do you know that? No one knows about that, and Andrew acted as if he'd gotten over me."

"Gotten over you?" Cassie grinned. "Oh sure, he tried to get over you, but his love for you is forever, and he still aches to tell you so."

"Is Andrew connected to my out-of-body experience?"

Cassie beamed. "Good for you! Keep connecting the dots."

19

DON'S LUNCHEONETTE

"There it is, Andrew!" Robin said. "There's Don's Luncheonette, left side on the corner."

Andrew turned into the parking lot. "Maybe that's Alex Olsen's vehicle."

"Yes, Alex said he drives a red pickup truck, and we'd probably see it."

Andrew parked next to the pickup, shut off the Impala's engine, and took a slow breath. "I feel this trip will be productive."

"Oh, so now you're getting intuitive feelings?" Robin quipped. "I thought that was my job."

The glass front door displayed the hours of operation. Andrew noted the Monday closing. As he peered inside the darkened interior, he could make out the figure of a middle-aged man moving around. "Someone's here. He's coming."

The brown-eyed, clean-shaven man who opened the door was slightly taller and heavier than Andrew. "I guess you must be Andrew and Robin. I'm Alex. Please come in."

Andrew extended a handshake. "Thank you for meeting with us today, Alex. I know Robin told you we are interested in finding Doreen Norton."

"Yes, she worked here when my brother and I were younger, when my dad was running the restaurant. After Doreen left, we heard she was pregnant. She worked well and was well-liked by the staff and customers. My dad liked her, but she wasn't here very long."

"We know Doreen's daughter, Clare, but she cannot travel right now," Andrew said. "She desperately wants to know about her mother. We hope your father will know something to help us find Doreen. Even the smallest tidbit of information might help."

"It will depend on how well Dad is doing. His dementia is progressing. You may waste your time if it's a bad day. Some days he barely responds. On good days, he talks about events that happened in the past. Sometimes he even thinks my mother is still alive."

Robin expressed empathy. "We understand, and we're sorry your father is dealing with that."

Andrew nodded supportively. "We can imagine it must be hard on you, your brother, and the rest of your family."

"Thank you," Alex said. "I just want you to understand the situation. My brother, David, will meet us there. We can leave now."

Andrew offered to drive, but Alex said, "Let's take my truck. The facility is close by. It will be better if we arrive before lunch."

During the short drive, Alex asked about Clare. "I guess Clare has been looking for her mother for a long time?"

"I believe so," Andrew said.

"If Clare cannot travel, does that mean she's ill?"

Andrew hesitated and glanced at Robin.

"She's in a coma," Robin said. "It's urgent we find Doreen because Clare's prognosis is poor. Clare had it tough growing up in foster care. The system shifted her around a lot, and she has had little stability in her adult life as well."

"I understand," Alex said.

Alex found a parking space in the third row in front of the main entrance. Andrew and Robin followed Alex into the building, where they found Don Olsen in the dayroom staring blankly at a television.

"Hey, Dad, I have some people who would like to talk to you. This is Andrew, and this is Robin."

The older gentleman took a few moments before turning to Robin. "Nancy? It *is* you! Get me out of here. Take me home. This is a terrible place!"

Robin spoke gently. "My name is Robin. Andrew and I want to talk to you. Do you want to talk to us?"

Alex whispered into Andrew's ear. "Nancy was my mom's name. Dad has mistaken Robin for my mother."

Don Olsen stared into space as if Robin had said nothing.

Robin persisted. "Mr. Olsen, do you remember a girl by the name of Doreen? She used to work for you at the luncheonette. It was a long time ago. We're hoping you can tell us about her. We must find her."

"Take me to my room," Mr. Olsen said. "Does anyone know the way to my room?"

"Sure, Dad," Alex said, signaling Andrew and Robin to follow him.

Out in the hallway, Andrew expressed his disappointment to Robin. "I'm afraid we're wasting our time. Don can't tell us anything."

"We'll see," Robin said with a smile.

They reached Mr. Olsen's room, and Alex positioned his dad's wheelchair to face the window with a view of the back lawn. No one spoke for several minutes. Andrew cast a disheartened glance in Robin's direction. Robin held up one finger to ask for patience.

Finally, Mr. Olsen spoke. "Robin, come around here where I can see you."

Andrew noticed Alex raise his eyebrows in utter amazement.

"Yes, Mr. Olsen," Robin said, moving into the man's line of sight.

"I got you mixed up with my wife a few minutes ago. My wife is dead."

"I know." Robin rested her backside on the windowsill. "I'm sorry about your wife. I know you had a good life together."

Mr. Olsen chuckled. "I just met you. How do you know we had a good life?"

"I know we've just met, but you have two fine sons and a good business. Your wife was a part of that, wasn't she?"

Mr. Olsen raised the corners of his lips. "Oh, that's what you meant. You know things, things about people, things others don't know."

Alex interrupted, "I'm sorry, but he's not having a good day."

Robin held Don Olsen's hand. "Quiet, please. We're connecting."

"Why do you want to find Doreen?" Mr. Olsen asked. "She quit a long time ago when she got pregnant. Doreen had a baby girl, but she gave up the baby."

"We know that, but Doreen's baby is now a grown woman and is looking for her," Robin said. "We want to reunite Doreen with her daughter. Did she ever come around again after she quit?"

"Yes. She visited the restaurant every year around my birthday."

"I never knew that," Alex said.

Robin continued. "That was very nice of her. When did you last see her? Do you remember?"

"Maybe it was five years ago. She stopped by because she was moving. She wanted to give me her new address."

"Do you know where she lives today?" Robin asked.

"The address is in my address book. Alex can find it for you. It's in my desk at the restaurant, bottom right-side drawer under the name of Doreen Allen."

"Is there anything else you can tell us, Mr. Olsen?" Andrew asked. "Anything at all?"

"Doreen got married to some kind of doctor, and together they had a daughter named Cassandra," Mr. Olsen said. "Cassandra passed away as a teenager."

"Did you ever meet Cassandra?" Robin asked.

Mr. Olsen nodded. "She was a beautiful girl, practically angelic."

"It must have been so hard on Doreen," Robin said, still in a kneeling position. "She gave up one daughter and lost another."

"It affected her. I think she will be happy to see her first daughter again. How old is she now?"

Andrew blurted, "She's thirty-four."

"Thank you, Mr. Olsen," Robin said, but as she let go of the elderly man's hand, he lost all focus. His eyes glazed over, and his mouth dropped half-open.

Alex called to his father. "Dad, Dad?" But there was no response.

Robin took Mr. Olsen's hand and tried to reconnect with him. "Mr. Olsen?" Again there was no response.

Alex sighed in frustration. "Well, that was the best he's been in quite a long time. I'm happy you two came all this way. It was good to have my father back." He looked at the clock on the wall of his dad's room. "I thought my brother would have been here by now. If you'd like, we can go back, and I will check my dad's desk for Doreen's address."

"Would you like to spend a little more time with him?" Andrew asked. "We can wait somewhere for you."

"Thanks, but that's okay. I'll let someone know he's here in his room. I'd like you to meet David too; he must be at the restaurant by now. But I think you're more interested in getting Doreen's address. If you're hungry, I can make a couple of burgers at the luncheonette. We can talk more, or if you are in a hurry, I'll just look for the address book, and you can go."

"We don't want to be any trouble," Robin said. "I know the luncheonette isn't open today."

"No problem!" Alex chuckled. "That's the beauty of it. You won't have to wait for a table."

Back at Don's Luncheonette, Alex told David about their father's brief mental clarity.

"Wow!" David exclaimed. "I think Dad's right. There is an address book in the drawer. It's old, and I've never looked at it."

Andrew and Robin waited with David while Alex headed into the back office. In just a minute or two, Alex emerged and said, "Got it! Here she is—Doreen Allen with an address in Spring Lake, New Jersey. I'll jot it down for you."

"By any chance," Andrew asked, "is there a telephone number too?"

"Afraid not," Alex said, handing him a slip of paper with the full address. "But I hope this helps." He gave the address book back to David.

Robin asked Andrew if he knew the Spring Lake area.

"Yes, it's a shore town with a boardwalk and Victorian homes. When I was little, my folks liked to go there just after Labor Day. By then, the summer crowd had gone, but the ocean water was still warm enough for swimming. After the beach, we'd grab something to eat, walk around, and look at the Victorian homes. Gosh, I haven't thought about that place in years."

Alex grinned. "It sounds so nice. You almost make me want to come with you to look for Doreen."

Andrew rubbed his chin. "That's not a bad idea. If Robin and I appear out of the blue, Doreen might not appreciate two strangers showing up."

Robin agreed. "I've been thinking the same thing. If our approach doesn't have the right finesse, we could get a door slammed in our faces. Doreen doesn't know us, so we can't predict how she'll react. Two unfamiliar people might upset her."

Andrew pressed Alex. "What do you say? I know it's a lot to ask, but come with us to Spring Lake. At least Doreen knows you from the past. No matter how it goes, I'll drive you back here tonight. It may make a big difference, and time is not on our side."

Inexplicably, Robin stood up and touched her head. "Excuse me. I need a little fresh air."

Concerned, Andrew followed. "Robin, Robin! Are you okay?"

Once outdoors, Robin leaned against Uncle Ed's Impala. "Don't talk." She took a couple of deep breaths, finally opening her eyes. "I'm okay, but I just got an extrasensory message from Don Olsen."

Andrew raised his eyebrows in disbelief.

"It only happened one other time," Robin said. "Even then, the message I received was from someone who had just passed away."

"Are you saying Mr. Olsen just passed away? We saw him not thirty minutes ago."

At that moment, Alex came out of the luncheonette and asked, "Is everything okay?"

"Yes, I'm fine," Robin said. "I just needed a little fresh air. I'm fine."

"Listen," Alex said, "I've got to run back to the nursing home. Dad has taken some sort of turn for the worse, but I can't get any more details until I get there. David is still inside, but I'm not sure whether we can entertain you with lunch, and I'm sorry, but I can't go to look for Doreen with you, at least not today. Stay in touch, though. I'd like to know if you find her."

"Don't worry about us," Andrew said. "We just hope everything will be okay with your father. Do what you have to do."

Alex extended a handshake to both. "Thanks. I've got to go."

Andrew waited for Alex to get in his truck and drive away before asking Robin, "So, do you think Mr. Olsen passed away?"

"I suspect so. All I know for sure is that I heard Mr. Olsen's voice inside my head."

"And what did Mr. Olsen's voice say?"

"He said he was with Nancy."

20

FINDING DOREEN

O nce Andrew and Robin had been back on the road for about twenty-five minutes, Robin suggested they stop for lunch and find a telephone. "Wouldn't it make more sense to call ahead instead of just showing up?"

Andrew checked traffic in the rearview mirror. "That's a good idea. Maybe we can find a diner with a pay phone and call information." He hung a sharp right that jostled Robin in the passenger seat. He chuckled. "Sorry, but I just saw a place."

The R & G Diner was a classic greasy spoon with rickety tables and plastic tablecloths. Inside the foyer, there were two public telephones and a coin-operated Captain Claw crane vending machine filled with stuffed toy prizes. Robin laughed and pointed at Captain Claw. "If you play, I predict you'll win something."

"Was that another Lady Nadia prediction?"

"No." Robin laughed. "It says right on the machine, 'Guaranteed Prize. Play Until You Win!'"

"That is funny!" Andrew rolled his eyes at her. "Do you want to get us a table while I see if I can get a number for Doreen?"

Robin shook her head. "No, I'll wait while you call."

Andrew pulled out a pen and used one of the pay phones to call directory assistance. There was no listing for either a Doreen Allen or a Doreen Norton, but there was a listing for a dermatologist named Dr. K. Michael Allen in Spring Lake, New Jersey.

Andrew jotted down the number and showed it to Robin.

"We know Doreen married a doctor," Robin said.

"That's what Don Olsen remembered, so let's see what happens when I call the office number."

A female voice answered, "Dr. Allen's office."

"Hello. My name is Andrew Leahy. I'm not sure if I have the right party."

"Sir, this is a dermatologist's office. You may have the wrong number."

Andrew cleared his throat. "That's very possible, but can I ask you something? I'm looking for a Doreen Allen."

The woman paused before she spoke again. "This is Doreen Allen. What is this about? Who did you say you are?"

Andrew mouthed the word *bingo* to Robin and returned his attention to Doreen. "My name is Andrew Leahy. Did you ever go by the name Doreen Norton?"

"Yes."

"And, as a teenager, did you work at Don's Luncheonette on Staten Island?"

Doreen answered abruptly, "I did. Exactly what do you want, Mr. Leahy?"

"Sorry, but I just needed to be sure I've found the right person. I've got some news, but it is personal. Would it be possible to meet with you?"

"Mr. Leahy," she said firmly, "I'm sure you'll understand that I don't know who you are. Perhaps if you just tell me now, and we'll take it from there."

Andrew hesitated a long moment. "May I call you Doreen?"

"Yes, fine."

Andrew's words were direct. "In 1952, you had a daughter and named her Clare. You were a teenager, and I understand you gave the baby up to the foster care system. Is that correct?"

Doreen sounded defensive. "I'm very busy at the moment."

"This is quite important," Andrew said. "I think once you hear what I have to tell you, you'll be interested."

Doreen continued to push Andrew away. "As I say, I am quite busy..."

Andrew thought it would be better to break it to Doreen gently, but he sensed Doreen was close to ending the call.

"I am sorry to tell you this, but Clare is in the hospital on life support. Her prognosis is poor. She asked me to find you because she'd wanted to meet you. Right now, unfortunately, she's lapsed into a coma, but even under these circumstances, I'm hoping you'd come to the hospital and visit her."

There was a long moment of silence coming from Doreen's end until she spoke again. "What is the nature of Clare's illness?"

"Apparently, it's a rare form of meningitis, very aggressive. Even if she were to emerge from the coma, it's unlikely she'll regain many functions."

"Oh, that is very upsetting. Yes, yes, I would like to see Clare."

Andrew felt a great sense of relief. "That's great, Doreen! But time is of the essence. I should tell you there's a meeting tomorrow about withdrawing life support. I don't know what kind of time-table we're talking about."

"Andrew, there is something I should tell you. I don't even know you, and I don't know why I feel the need to tell you this, but I never told my husband that I gave a baby up as a teenager. Maybe I should have told him, but I never did. Whatever happens, may I ask you to keep that to yourself?"

"Of course, I understand."

"My husband is a doctor here in Spring Lake, and I work as his receptionist. I'm scheduled to work tomorrow, but I think I can find someone to cover for me. Would it be possible for me to see Clare tomorrow?"

"Yes, come tomorrow, but now I have something to tell you. The hospital staff thinks I'm Clare's brother. I had to say that, or they would have prevented me from seeing her because of the hospital's visitor policy. I'm trying to keep up that ploy as long as I can. It may help to get you in as well. I think that's a better strategy than if you appeared out of nowhere and claimed to be her biological mother."

"What is your relationship with Clare?"

Andrew maintained a manner-of-fact tone. "We're friends, old college classmates. She once asked me to help her find her biological mother, and that's why I'm doing this."

"I have so many questions about her life, but I cannot talk anymore right now. I've got a patient standing in front of me and another call on hold."

"I understand. I'm staying with my uncle. His name is Ed. Call me there when you're free to talk." Andrew recited Uncle Ed's phone number.

After Andrew hung up, Robin said, "That sounded as if it went well."

Andrew nodded. "Doreen wants to see Clare. The only hitch is she never told her husband she gave up a baby, and she wants to keep that a secret."

Back on the road after a quick lunch, Robin said, "The fact that Doreen never told her husband about Clare may have something to do with why the Universe wants to reunite Doreen and Clare. Maybe there's some sort of unfinished business between Doreen and Dr. Allen."

"That's possible."

"And we should call the Olsen brothers, too," Robin said. "I'm still thinking about the message I got from their father."

21

ANDREW'S DREAM

That evening, while Uncle Ed prepared a spaghetti dinner and Robin made a salad, Andrew split his time on the telephone between Alex Olsen and Doreen Allen. When he finally finished his call with Doreen, he felt a wave of fatigue wash over him. It had been a draining day. Maybe a plate of his uncle's spaghetti with meat sauce would be the pick-me-up he needed.

Uncle Ed called Andrew to the table. "We're almost ready. If you're off the phone, you can start with salad."

Robin placed a bowl of fresh garden salad on the table. "Be right back with the dressing. I made it from scratch." A moment later, she returned with a half-filled jar of homemade dressing.

"How was your day, Andrew?" Uncle Ed asked. "Did you find the person you were searching for?"

After bringing his uncle up to speed, Andrew said, "I just got off the phone with Don Olsen's son, Alex, and unfortunately, Don passed away shortly after we saw him." He omitted the detail about Robin psychically hearing Don Olsen say he was with his wife, Nancy.

"What happened?" Uncle Ed asked.

"Alex said it was probably a massive stroke."

"How are Alex and David doing?" Robin asked.

"Handling it, I suppose. They thank us for going out there."

"Did you tell Alex we contacted Doreen?" Robin asked.

"Yes and when I spoke to Doreen, I told her about Don as well."

Uncle Ed stopped eating for a moment. "And things aren't looking good for your friend, Clare?"

"I'm afraid there's little hope, Uncle Ed. If she survives, she'll have no quality of life, according to the doctor."

Andrew said to Robin, "I explained to Doreen more about how I know Clare, and that Clare is divorcing Jason Rinaldi and now lives with Sam Agnellini."

"Did you tell Doreen anything about Clare's relationship with either of them?" Robin asked before she sipped from a glass of water.

"If Doreen hadn't asked, I wouldn't have brought it up," Andrew said. "I told her Jason cheated on her, and I shared my opinion of Sam."

At the end of the meal, Andrew stifled a yawn. "Thank you, Uncle Ed. If nobody needs me for anything, I'm feeling a little sleepy, and I'm going to rest my eyes on the couch." The last thing he heard was Robin loading the dishwasher. Straightaway, he fell into a deep sleep with thoughts of Clare covering him like a warm, comforting blanket.

In his dream, it was evening, and Andrew was on a tapered dirt road in deep green woods. The sun's rays hid behind a cloud, hurrying the night along. He heard some rustling in the underbrush, which he thought might be the forest's nocturnal animals becoming active. The next sound he heard was that of a vintage, yellow and black horse-drawn carriage rolling over some rutted roots.

A tall, thin driver with a scraggly beard called to the horse, "Whoa, Prince! I suppose this fellow must be the one."

Andrew took a moment to admire the sleek, chestnut-colored stallion. "Did you call him Prince?"

"Yes, and Prince is here for you."

"Is he?" Andrew asked, thoroughly taken aback.

"Pet him if you like. He already knows all about you."

"Excuse me, but I've never seen the horse before. He seems like a superb animal, but I'm afraid you're mistaken. I neither know Prince nor do I know who you are."

The man laughed as if he'd heard a joke. "Mistaken? You must understand. There are no mistakes here, Andrew. Not in this place."

"Where am I? Who are you? How do you know my name?"

"It is perfectly understandable that you have so many questions, Andrew. May I invite you to join me on the carriage seat that I might provide at least some of your answers?" He chuckled. "Other answers are for you to discover."

Andrew accepted the man's invitation.

"My name is Jerome. Make yourself comfortable, Andrew Leahy from South Amboy, or should I say Sugarloaf Key?" He paused. "That's part of your conundrum, isn't it?"

"Oh, is this about my decision whether to go on tour?"

"No, but that's a good guess," Jerome said, tugging on his beard. "The Universe has given you the gift of music, and I hope you'll use your gift, but that's not why you're here. You're here because of Clare."

"Do you know Clare?"

"Everyone here knows Clare!"

"Even Prince?"

"Especially Prince," the man whispered as if telling a secret. "Prince will take you to her."

Andrew wondered if he had suffered a fatal heart attack right on Uncle Ed's couch and gone to the afterlife. "Is this a way station on the way to heaven?"

"No, but that's another good guess. In the physical world, you are asleep on your uncle's couch, and Clare's body is in the hospital bed. You are in the spirit realm to see Clare. She's just down this road at the edge of the water. I thought you might enjoy taking Clare for a ride around the lake."

"Does this mean I'm dreaming about taking Clare for a buggy ride?"

Jerome elbowed Andrew's ribs. "This isn't just any carriage. It's a courting carriage, and besides, we do some of our best work through dreams."

"Who are *we*?" Andrew asked, but the mysterious man disappeared without answering.

Prince knew the way, so Andrew relaxed and inhaled the woodsy fragrance that permeated the air. Even in the fading light, the green and brown colors appeared more vivid, and the sound of the breeze rustling through the trees inspired a feeling of tranquility. The trail opened to a clearing, where he saw her at the edge of an oval lake.

Clare turned to face the advancing courting carriage. She sounded genuinely pleased when she spoke his name. "Andrew?"

Fumbling his words, he uttered, "Yeah, it's me, and this is my new friend, Prince."

"Prince is beautiful!"

"So are you," Andrew said, climbing down from the carriage and embracing Clare. "Are you surprised to see me?"

Clare chuckled. "Not really. I'm happy to see you, but not surprised. Everything that happens here has a purpose."

"Would you join me for a carriage ride around the lake? Prince knows the way, so I'm told."

"Did Prince tell you that?" Clare giggled.

"A man named Jerome told me that."

"Oh, you've met Jerome, a tall guy with somewhat of an untidy beard? He's been my spirit guide from the beginning of all of this."

Andrew offered his hand and helped Clare up on the carriage. "Yeah, that must be the guy."

Clare accepted Andrew's help, and in a moment, they sat close together, and the carriage moved forward at a gentle pace under Prince's power.

"According to Jerome, I'm asleep on my uncle's couch, and you are still in a coma at the hospital, and yet here we are." He continued to make small talk before he realized he was avoiding the chance to tell Clare of his feelings for her.

Prince sensed Andrew's hesitation and stopped to eat some grass on the side of the trail. Andrew got the horse's message. "Clare, I think I know why I'm here. I'm here to talk to you, and I've prayed for this chance." Andrew took Clare's hand. "Just listen, at least to me. What I have to say is important."

Clare's eyes met Andrew's, and she squeezed his hand in hers. "Okay, I'm listening."

Andrew didn't want to leave out any detail. "I'm going to start at the beginning. On our first day of classes, I noticed you sitting at the second desk in the first row next to the wall. When I walked into the classroom, you were engaged in conversation with another student, talking about high school. I was already so enthralled with you that I couldn't say much. You hit me like a runaway train, a train I never saw coming."

. "Being hit by a train, isn't that a violent image?"

Andrew shrugged. "Maybe, but being hit by an oncoming train has a powerful suddenness. It changes one's life in an instant. From the first moment I saw you, everything changed. At the end of class, I went to my car and just sat there wondering what had just happened to me."

"What are you saying, Andrew?"

"I'm saying the truth. I love you."

It was four o'clock in the morning when Andrew woke up and realized Uncle Ed and Robin had left him on the couch overnight. He tried to go back to sleep so he could return to Clare, but he was too wide awake. Andrew found a tablet and sketched out the details of his dream. His notes expressed frustration because he didn't get a chance to gauge Clare's response to what he'd said to her.

Later that morning, after Uncle Ed had left for work, Andrew described the strange dream to Robin over a second cup of coffee. "It felt so good expressing my feelings, but I feel frustrated too because I want to tell her more."

"Didn't you say you often have dreams about Clare? Were you in another realm, or just dreaming?"

"Hmm, I guess I can't be sure," Andrew admitted. "The dream was vivid, though."

"Dreams fulfill people's unconscious desires," Robin said.

"Since when did Lady Nadia turn into Sigmund Freud?"

"I didn't." Robin chuckled. "All I'm saying is the mind is vulnerable to suggestion."

"What about the horse and carriage? Did my unconscious come up with that?"

"Riding in a carriage may symbolize a slow and difficult journey."

"There was nothing difficult about the carriage ride."

"Have the last fifteen years been difficult for you?"

Andrew nodded. "Yes."

Robin shook her head. "Maybe we can't agree on this, but one thing we can agree on is that this total experience has been highly unusual, even for *Key West's most gifted psychic*."

Their discussion was interrupted by a phone call from Dr. Siegel.

22

CHANGE IN NEUROLOGICAL STATUS

"There's a change in Clare's neurological status," Dr. Siegel said.

Andrew feared it was bad news. "What is it?"

"She opened her eyes, which, given her condition, is a miracle."

"That's wonderful!" Andrew exclaimed. He turned to Robin and said, "Clare is awake!"

"She isn't following people or objects with her eyes, and she's not responding to auditory or tactile stimuli."

Andrew's heart sank. "Is there anything else?"

Dr. Siegel offered other good news. "Clare is no longer on a respirator. She's breathing on her own."

"Can Clare understand what's being said to her?"

"I see no evidence of language comprehension," Dr. Siegel said, "but we may see changes in that area."

"I know you can't predict," Andrew said, "but in your experience, how much of a recovery could someone make in Clare's situation?"

"It's difficult to accept, but in my honest medical opinion," Dr. Siegel said, "the odds of Clare making a full recovery are at best two percent."

"Will we still meet tomorrow?"

"Yes," Dr. Siegel said. "We'll be in Conference Room 401, but I have to move the time to 3:45 p.m. I want to give all concerned parties a chance to understand your sister's prognosis. Right now, it's a wait-and-see proposition. Things could change or stay the same. Do you have any other questions?"

"No questions," Andrew said, "but before Clare got sick, she asked me to locate her biological mother, Doreen Allen. Doreen knows about Clare's medical situation, and I'm bringing her to the hospital tomorrow. I hope that will be all right."

"I understand, and that's fine."

Relieved the physician didn't ask for more details, Andrew thanked Dr. Siegel. "Please call me if there are any other developments. Otherwise, I'll see you tomorrow."

Andrew recapped what Dr. Siegel had just told him. He regarded Robin, who remained quiet. Finally, he asked, "What are you thinking?"

"Stay positive," Robin said.

Andrew understood what Robin meant, and he knew he should remain grateful for every small step in the right direction.

"You should call Doreen Allen and let her know," Robin said. Just then, the telephone rang again. "I bet that's her."

Andrew answered, "Hello."

"Is this Andrew? This is Doreen Allen."

Andrew nodded to Robin. "Yes, good morning, Doreen."

"I'm not sure I can make it to the hospital today," Doreen said, "but I may get there tonight around eight. Do you think I'll be able to see Clare then?"

"I don't think so. Visiting hours end at eight o'clock, but first, there's something I have to tell you. Clare opened her eyes. She's awake, but the doctor doesn't know what additional improvement we may see." Andrew thought he heard sobbing. "Are you okay?"

"Yes, yes."

"Can I make a suggestion?" Andrew asked.

Doreen's voice was just above a whisper. "What is it?"

"The meeting will be in the afternoon. What would you say about having lunch here at my uncle's house at one o'clock? Afterward, we can go to the hospital for the meeting."

Doreen agreed. "I'll find someone to cover for me."

Andrew gave her the address and directions. "Ours is the only house on North Point Road."

Andrew hung up and said to Robin, "From the way Doreen sounded, I suspect she hasn't told her husband about Clare yet."

"Although the Universe may want us to bring Doreen and Clare together, the onus is on Doreen regarding what she tells Dr. Allen."

"Another one of those midcourse corrections you're always talking about?"

"Doreen is being deceitful by omission. That's not good."

Andrew smiled knowingly. "I'd like to visit Clare by myself, Robin. I hope you don't mind staying alone this morning,"

Robin smiled. "I don't mind."

"I could drop you downtown if you want a break."

"I'll be all right here. Go spend time with Clare."

"Doreen is coming here for lunch tomorrow. Would you help me with that? We can shop when I get back."

"Sure, Andrew," Robin agreed. "I'll make a list."

Andrew stopped at Judy's Flower Pot to shop for flowers.

The florist made a bouquet of Asiatic and Peruvian lilies and sunflowers. "How about pink roses and carnations?" she asked.

"Sure."

She continued accenting the arrangement with assorted greenery and lavender and purple colors, all artistically designed in a green vase, which evoked the life-affirming feeling Andrew wanted it to convey.

At the hospital, Andrew intended to stop at the nursing station, but he changed his mind and went directly into Clare's room. Her condition was as Dr. Siegel had described. Still, he wondered if she could hear him or if she even knew he was there.

"Clare, it is Andrew. I brought you some flowers. I hope you like them." He set the flower arrangement on the windowsill, away from Clare's bed. "I had this crazy dream last night that you and I were taking a carriage ride, being pulled by a horse named Prince. We went around a beautiful lake, so idyllic. The dream seemed real."

Andrew paused for several moments. "And in the dream, Clare, I told you I love you, but I guess it was only a dream."

The moment was interrupted by a mature, poker-faced nurse. "Did you bring those flowers?"

Even though he believed he had done nothing wrong, the nurse's tone made Andrew feel guilty. "Yes."

"You can't bring flowers into an intensive care room. It's against the policy, so please remove them. Patients here are too sick."

"I understand." He waited for the nurse to perform her tasks before saying goodbye to Clare. The nurse motioned toward the flowers; Andrew smiled his intent to comply before returning his attention to Clare.

He realized the staff must have removed the previous flowers and shrugged his shoulders. "Rules are rules. I'd better do as I'm told." He leaned down, kissed her cheek, and promised he'd be back. Andrew considered what Dr. Siegel had said about Clare's poor prognosis. He whispered his questions to the Universe as much as to Clare. "Why did you come to me, Clare? I'm the only one who can see you. I don't understand."

23

MOTHER AND CHILD REUNION

oreen arrived at the Leahy residence the next day at one o'clock in the afternoon. She got out of her car as Andrew stepped onto the porch to welcome her. Dressed in dark-blue slacks and a white ruffled blouse, Doreen moved with the fluidity of a younger woman. "Andrew? It's nice to meet you. I'm Doreen."

"Thanks so much for coming," Andrew said. "I thought we could get together before we meet with the doctor. I have to explain a few things to avoid any awkwardness later. Let's go inside."

"One second," Doreen said. "I have a cake in the car."

"That's so nice of you."

"It's from a very good bakery near where I live. It's not home-made, but I hope you like it."

Once inside the house, Robin came out from the kitchen. "Hello! I'm Andrew's friend, Robin."

Doreen passed the boxed cake to Robin. "It's a Black Forest cake from my favorite bakery."

After the initial pleasantries, Andrew invited Doreen to sit at the dining room table, and Robin brought out a large bowl of salad.

Doreen sprinkled a little of the homemade dressing onto her salad and began asking questions. "Andrew, I understand you were friends with Clare in college and that you lost track of her for a long time. How did you reconnect with her?"

Andrew couldn't tell Doreen that Clare's spirit had appeared on his doorstep. He answered by saying, "A friend told me she was sick, so I came back home to see if there was anything I could do."

"And you told the hospital you are Clare's brother so you'd be able to see her?"

"That's right, which brings up a delicate point. I'd prefer to maintain that story so I can continue to visit Clare, and I don't want to be caught in a lie."

Doreen put down her fork. "Does that mean I'm your mother? I mean, if I'm going along with your lie, we better get our facts straight."

Andrew looked at Robin while he processed the idea. "Maybe I could be Clare's younger half brother. If anyone asks, we'll say Doreen had me a year after she gave up Clare."

Robin rolled her eyes. "Do you think anyone will ask?"

Doreen agreed. "I think Robin is right. No one will ask, and if anyone does, I'll go along with anything Andrew says."

"Doreen, tell us a little about you. What happened after you gave up Clare?" Robin asked.

"I was just a teenager when I got pregnant," Doreen said. "Clare's father was a gang member. He stole cars. We talked of marriage and family, you know, a normal life, but a rival gang killed him. Paul was his name. He never knew about Clare. I was such an emotional mess. I don't know how I even finished school, but I did."

"That's tragic," Robin said.

"After high school, I got into a two-year college program, but I stopped my formal education at that point and got a job at the local hospital. That's where I met Michael, my husband. He asked me to do some administrative work in his Staten Island office. This turned into a full-time job. Michael moved his practice to Spring Lake. We ended up getting married."

Robin probed further. "Tell us about your time at Don's Luncheonette."

"My employment there was less than two years," Doreen said. "I left before my pregnancy showed, hoping to give up the baby and keep everything secret. Word got around, and I became the subject of gossip."

Robin phrased her next question with caution. "Doreen, this is none of our business, so you don't have to answer, but we know you never told your husband about Clare. Why is that?"

Doreen's answer was candid. "Early on, we had an employer-employee relationship, so it was of no concern. After we became romantic, I didn't want Michael to judge me. Later, I thought too much time had gone by, so it didn't matter. He knows nothing about Clare's father's death either. Michael knows I grew up in a rough neighborhood with little money. I tried not to portray my life more colorfully than necessary. None of that is important now."

"On the contrary, it may be very important now. How have you handled keeping Clare's birth a secret?"

"By keeping quiet about it," Doreen said.

Robin continued, "It must take a lot of energy to hold that secret in."

Andrew wasn't sure why Robin was doing this. He shook his head at her as if to tell her to stop.

"I'm sorry," Robin said. "This is none of our business. Let's finish lunch and head over to the hospital."

There was an uncomfortable silence before Doreen spoke again. "Robin is right. It takes a lot of energy to keep a secret like that. Should I tell him?"

"We are not telling you what you should or shouldn't do," Robin said. "It's up to you to decide, or maybe you've already decided. The only reason I brought it up is that I sense you feel as if you've made a mistake, and you are looking to correct it."

"I don't know what caused you to bring this up, but I'm glad you did. It's an amazing coincidence that Clare should come back to me now."

Andrew took a sip of water. "Robin doesn't believe in coincidences. I'm getting so I don't either." He considered sharing the whole Clare-out-of-body account with Doreen, but he decided it was too early for that.

"I don't mean to rush anybody," Doreen said, "but we should go to the hospital."

Andrew, Robin, and Doreen arrived at the hospital forty-five minutes before the scheduled meeting. This allowed Doreen to spend a few minutes with Clare. Because of the ICU's limit on visitors, Andrew accompanied Doreen into Clare's room while Robin waited in a lounge down the hall.

Entering Clare's room, Doreen walked in a few steps ahead of Andrew. She stopped an arm's length from the bedside.

"This must be hard for you," Andrew whispered.

"Yes, it is."

"Doreen, why don't you introduce yourself?" Andrew suggested.

"Can she hear me? Will she understand me?"

"I don't know, but I've been speaking to her, and it has given me some sense of connection to her."

Doreen stepped forward and touched Clare's hand. "Clare, I'm your mother. I know you've been looking for me. You must have so many questions about why I didn't keep you. It's because I was only a teenager, and I couldn't have supported you. Your father died, and my parents didn't want me to bring you home. I didn't know what to do." Doreen lowered her eyes and exited the room.

Robin leaned into the doorway. "Dr. Siegel is ready to start the meeting. Everyone is in a conference room."

24

DR. SIEGEL

Friday, May 10, 1985

Doreen waited for Andrew and Robin in the hallway. Together, the trio entered the conference room, led by Andrew.

Dr. Siegel introduced himself as the neurologist in charge of Clare's case. "Please go around the table and introduce yourselves. Can we start on my right?"

Before the two men on the opposite side of the table even made their introductions, Andrew distinguished Jason from Sam. Jason was straight out of central casting: black T-shirt and navy-blue suit. He sported a feathered shag hairstyle, and had blue eyes and white teeth. Sam carried some fatty body weight and wore a slicked-back hairstyle.

"Well, I'm Jason Rinaldi, Clare's husband."

The next person said, "Sam Agnellini here. Clare works at my restaurant." He shifted his body in the cushioned conference chair before adding, "We live together and were planning to get married once the courts complete our divorces."

Robin smiled. "I'm Robin McGovern, Clare's sister-in-law."

"Andrew McGovern, her brother."

"Doreen Allen, Clare's mother."

"Excuse me," Jason said. "Clare's mother? Clare's brother? Who are these people? Clare grew up in foster care. She has no family!"

Doreen answered with equal energy, "I know I gave up my rights years ago, and I have my regrets about that, but I *am* Clare's biological mother. If it's okay with everyone else, I just want to be here."

"And you?" Jason directed his attention to Andrew. "You say you are Clare's brother?"

"That's right. I'm her younger half brother." Andrew gestured to Doreen. "This is my mom."

Sam picked up on something that could expose the truth about Andrew. "If you're Clare's *half* brother, and this woman is your mother, why are you and Clare both going by the name of McGovern? If you had different fathers, you should have a different last name."

Robin distracted from Jason and Sam's questions by saying, "We can get into this later. Dr. Siegel's time is valuable, and I'm sure we're all here because we are concerned about Clare's health."

"Yes, Dr. Siegel," Andrew said, picking up on Robin's lead. "We can hash this out later, so please tell us about Clare."

"Of course," the physician agreed. "I want to update you on Clare's condition."

"Is Clare gonna get better?" Sam interrupted.

Dr. Siegel referred to a file as he spoke. "Clare collapsed on the floor in the restaurant where she works."

Sam raised his hand. "That's my restaurant. Clare works in my restaurant. We called the first aid squad."

Dr. Siegel tapped his pen on the table as if calling for order. "Clare came into our emergency department on Monday, May 6. She experienced a grand mal seizure in the ambulance and was unconscious upon arrival. We did a CT scan of the head and a lumbar puncture. The diagnosis was bacterial meningitis, and she began receiving intravenous antibiotics. After an hour, we found it necessary to place her on a ventilator."

Again, Sam interrupted. "Well, she's not on a ventilator anymore. That's significant, right?"

Jason unclasped his hands and gestured toward Dr. Siegel with his index finger. "Let the doctor finish, will you, man?"

Dr. Siegel maintained his professionalism. "I want everyone to understand the seriousness of Clare's status. There won't be much more improvement. Yes, the fact that she's off mechanical ventilation is significant, but we may not see much more improvement. Her vital signs are stable, and if that continues, we can move her to a long-term care facility."

Doreen sobbed. "Can Clare hear me when I speak to her?"

"Perhaps," Dr. Siegel said, "but the infection attacked her cerebral cortex. The cerebral cortex is the outer portion of the brain where conscious thoughts take place. It is the part of the brain that makes us all human. In Clare's case, the infection damaged the cerebral cortex."

"Sounds bad," Sam muttered.

Dr. Siegel continued. "When Dr. Youngman did the lumbar puncture in the emergency room, thick pus came out. All of the scans we've done throughout the week have shown the infection has bathed her brain in pus."

Sam's next question to the doctor made Andrew cringe. "Should we be talking about letting her go?"

"When I contacted all of you for this meeting," Dr. Siegel said, "I intended to discuss removing Clare from the mechanical life support, but as you all know, she is now breathing on her own. Therefore, we can continue to care for her until moving her to another facility."

"Excuse me, Dr. Siegel," Robin said, "but what's the worst-case scenario?"

Dr. Siegel nodded as if he had already intended to address that question. "Although I think we will transfer her for long-term care, it is still possible Clare could take a turn for the worse, and we could lose her."

"Have you discontinued sedation now that she is no longer intubated?" Robin asked.

"Yes, but it's still in her system."

"Will she have more awareness when the sedation wears off?" Andrew asked.

"It's possible," Dr. Siegel said, "but it may not be enough to change the overall picture."

Jason fidgeted in his chair. "It sounds like we have to just wait and see."

"Correct." Dr. Siegel nodded.

Sam shook his head and muttered, "Well, I have a restaurant to run. You know where to reach me."

"I guess that's it for me too," Jason said, "unless there's anything else, Doctor."

Dr. Siegel stood up to leave as well, his eyes on Doreen. "Thank you for coming in. When you visit Clare, it would be good if you announced your presence. Tell her about your day. Touch her. Hold her hand. Even if she doesn't seem to respond, you will still comfort her."

Jason shook hands with everyone. "Clare is a beautiful person, and even though our marriage didn't work out, I'm sorry this is happening."

Walking out of the hospital, Doreen was circumspect. "I don't know how this will go, but I have to tell Michael about Clare."

25

THE DISCHARGE PLAN

A ndrew stayed in South Amboy longer than he'd intended because he wanted to see what would happen with Clare. During one of his daytime visits, he noticed Clare's eyes reacting when he spoke to her, and she appeared to be trying to respond.

When Dr. Siegel came in during his routine rounds, he examined Clare and didn't think she had any meaningful awareness. "Clare may hear us, but I doubt she understands us. Keep talking to her, though."

"All right, Doctor."

"I'm sure you've heard that your mother wants to move Clare to a facility in the Spring Lake area."

Andrew hadn't heard from Doreen and meant to call her soon. "That's news to me. I haven't spoken to Mom since the day of our meeting."

"Oh?"

"I'll call her tonight, but what's the plan?"

"Your mother came in with her husband, a Dr. Allen," Dr. Siegel explained. "I understand Dr. Allen isn't your father, but he's quite an amiable man from what I can tell. Mrs. Allen wants to assume responsibility for Clare's care. Given Mr. Rinaldi and Clare are divorcing and Mr. Agnellini saying he can't do much, Mrs. Allen presents a suitable alternative. Sorry if I've left you out of the loop, but your mom tells me you're from out of state, and she doubts you'd be available to take on this responsibility. Are you all right with this?"

Andrew took a moment to answer before nodding his head. "Yes, it sounds all right to me."

"Very good! We should be ready to transfer her on Friday."

After a brief visit with Clare, Andrew returned to Uncle Ed's, eager to share this recent development with Robin. "I have an important update about Clare," he said, coming through the front door.

"Hold that thought. I think we're witnessing a cosmic shift in the Universe."

"A cosmic shift in the Universe," Andrew repeated. "Robin, you're the only person who would start a conversation that way."

"Guess who I just got off the phone with!" Robin exclaimed.

"Doreen Allen?"

"Correct! Did she reach you at the hospital?"

"No, I talked to Dr. Siegel. He told me Doreen brought her husband to the hospital, and they've developed this plan in which Doreen will be responsible for Clare while she's in a long-term care facility."

"Doreen's husband is very supportive."

Andrew thought it must be a relief for Doreen. "It stressed her all these years."

"Giving up a newborn has weighed on Doreen," Robin said. "Plus, she's hidden that part of her life from her husband. I'd say, yeah, it is a relief."

Instead of sharing Robin's excitement, Andrew felt something akin to grief. He emptied the contents of his pockets and slumped onto the sofa. "I guess that's it."

"What's it?"

"The reason Clare's spirit came to me was to bring her and her mother back together." He shrugged. "I was selfish to think this would bring me and Clare together."

"Maybe so, Andrew, but you would have done it anyway. Don't think of yourself as selfish. You put your life and your music career on hold. That's not selfishness."

"My motive was selfish."

"Things will be okay. Now Clare has her mom back, and Doreen has her daughter. The tumblers have clicked into place."

Robin's choice of words confused Andrew. "Tumblers?"

"It means the Universe has self-corrected. We've brought Clare and Doreen together, and I think Doreen has done whatever healing she had to do with her husband."

"Is that it? Is that the reason Clare's spirit came to me?"

Robin smiled more with her eyes than with her lips. "You've been hoping the Universe sent Clare back into your life so you and Clare could be together."

"That's what I had hoped."

Robin was steadfast. "You performed an act of unselfish love."

Andrew sighed. "I guess our work here is done. It's time to go back to Key West."

"I think we've done everything we can do. Your role has been very special. We don't know what will happen to Clare, but she'll get the care she needs. Let's pray Doreen finds some peace."

"I'm happy for Doreen," Andrew said, "but I have a funny feeling this isn't over for me."

26

RECOVERING MEMORIES

C lare would later compare coming out of the coma to resting in a kelp bed. It was like seeing shafts of light beaming down through a dense canopy of large, tree-like plants in shallow ocean water. She knew she needed to get to the surface.

Early in her recovery, she had no language comprehension, no words to represent items like *bed*, *food*, or *tray*. Clare could neither recognize people nor even understand she was in a hospital. She focused on a female figure next to the bed who said she was her mother. Although she didn't know what *mother* meant, she knew how it felt. *Mother*—it carried a positive vibration.

After many arduous therapy sessions, Clare defied medical expectations and regained her physical and cognitive capacities. Sitting in the sunny courtyard, Doreen asked Clare if she remembered anything about the coma.

"I had a strange dream."

"What do you remember about this dream?"

First, Clare described the strange customer and how he'd told her she was about to have a transformative experience. "I didn't understand, but I was already sick and may not have heard him right. I remember he left his umbrella, which I put in our lost-and-found closet."

"You had a life-altering experience," Doreen agreed.

"Wait! It gets weirder. The customer appeared in my dream."

"Then what happened?"

"My customer turned into a doctor, and his name was Dr. Emiliani—only he wasn't an actual doctor. He said was my spirit guide and I should call him Jerome."

Doreen shook her head. "This customer from the restaurant shows up in your dream? Dreams can be so fragmented and illogical."

Clare told Doreen that she would dematerialize from one place and reappear in another. "One time, I was on a beach. When I knocked on a door to ask for help, the person who answered was a former college classmate named Andrew Leahy. Andrew was the only one who could see me in spirit form. My physical body was in a coma at the hospital."

"Huh?" Doreen paused. "Who was in this dream?"

"Just a friend from college. I haven't seen him in years, and I don't know why I would dream of him."

"Andrew Leahy and his girlfriend, Robin, were the ones who tracked me down and reunited me with you."

"That's amazing! Only I don't think they're a couple. Robin is Andrew's friend. She's his sidekick and helper. They know each other from Key West. At least that's the way it was in my dream."

Moments later, Clare because distracted by a small bird. The robin hopped toward her on thin black legs. "I know this bird. This robin was in my dream too, and he sang his song at my hospital window while I was in a coma."

"Dr. Siegel said you could not have had any consciousness, considering your neuro status. Your brain was too sick for dreams."

Clare laughed when the robin started clicking his tongue at Doreen. "The bird says I'm right. This is the robin from my dream."

At that moment, the memory of meeting her father in the garden warmed Clare's heart. "Mom, tell me about Paul McGovern."

Doreen's mouth dropped open. "Clare, how do you know that name? Your friend, Andrew, must be an excellent investigator."

Clare shook her head. "No, it wasn't Andrew. Paul told me himself. He said he had a nickname too—Kid Switchblade. You gave me his surname—McGovern—didn't you? He was in a gang, but he died when another gang ambushed him. They used his knife to slit his throat."

Doreen paced around the courtyard, her hands shaking. Finally, she said, "I haven't thought of Paul's nickname in years. Perhaps Andrew and Robin tracked down Paul's mother, and she told them. That would be your paternal grandmother, your biological grandmother, that is. I believe she remained in the same house on Staten Island."

"No, Paul told me his nickname, and do you know what this means? My coma-dream wasn't a dream. It was real. It also means I have a family in this world. I've always felt so alone, but knowing I have family out there gives me a sense of home. I've never had that before."

"Sorry if I don't believe you," Doreen said, "but your biological father could not have come to you in a dream. According to Dr. Siegel, the infection damaged your brain so that you could not have dreamed."

Clare was blunt. "I'm not crazy. I was in a coma, and I had an unusual experience, an experience I can't explain. Each day I remember more details. One of these days, I'm going to put it together and understand what it all means."

27

THE (NEW?) OVERSEAS HIGHWAYMEN

THURSDAY, MAY 30, 1985

A ndrew was in for a surprise when he telephoned Camp Turtle Cove to confirm the band's appearance at its third annual fundraiser.

A female voice picked up Andrew's call, "Turtle Cove."

"This is Andrew Leahy of the Overseas Highwaymen. May I speak to Mr. Harris?"

"Hold please, Mr. Leahy."

"Thank you."

Harris got on the line. "Mr. Leahy! How are you, sir?"

"I'm very well, Mr. Harris. I won't take but a minute, but I just want to confirm our performance time on Saturday. Is it still four o'clock?"

"I'm afraid you have me at a disadvantage. It's my understanding you are no longer with the band."

"Beg your pardon, but what are you talking about?"

"I understood that you and your bass player left, and the remaining members are reconstituting the band."

"Sorry, but I don't understand."

"The band is now *Alan Browne's Overseas Highwaymen*. They want to use the camp's fundraiser as a springboard for their new direction. It's been a well-kept secret from the media."

"A well-kept secret, huh?"

"The new band members are all very young and very talented. They're bringing in a horn section, from what I hear."

"By any chance have you spoken to Gary Feld?"

"No, I haven't."

"There must be some misunderstanding!"

"I'm sorry if you're hearing this for the first time," Mr. Harris said.

Andrew didn't know what was happening. "I'll get back to you. I have to make some more calls now."

As soon as he hung up with Mr. Harris, Andrew called Gary Feld. "Gary, this is Andrew. What's happening with the band?"

"Andrew!" Gary exclaimed. "What's going on, man? Where are you?"

"I'm home, but what about the band?"

"Oh, not much is happening. The guys say they're busy. We haven't rehearsed in a couple of weeks."

"Gary, I just got off the phone with Mr. Harris over at Camp Turtle Cove. He told me the Overseas Highwaymen changed its name to Alan Browne's Overseas Highwaymen. What do you know about that?"

"I don't know what you're talking about! We're still scheduled to play at the camp on Saturday as the Overseas Highwaymen, and since you're back, we should get in a rehearsal beforehand. Do you want me to set it up?"

"Hold off on that until I talk to Alan. Maybe Mr. Harris misunderstood something, although I don't know why he thinks we're bringing in a horn section."

"Everything is okay, Andrew. We missed a couple of gigs, and Alan notified the venues. No fallout from that, I guess. Otherwise, nothing has changed since you left a month ago. The guys will be glad to know you're back."

That day, Andrew attempted to reach both Alan Browne and Billy Morris by telephone but got no response. Frustrated, he drove into Key West, where Alan and Billy rented separate condos in the same building; he couldn't find either of them at home. By late afternoon, Andrew was feeling tired, frustrated, and hungry, so he stopped at Robin's to see how she was settling back in.

Andrew updated her on his phone calls with Gary and Mr. Harris, and his attempt to find Alan and Billy in person. "I should have stayed more closely in contact with them while we were away. Instead, I trusted Gary to be my liaison because I didn't want anyone to know where we'd gone, and I didn't want to be hit with a lot of questions."

Andrew had an idea. "Let's drive out to the Backwaters. We can get something to eat, and Thursday is their open mic/jam night. It might be fun." The Backwaters Grille & Tiki Bar was one gig the band missed while he was in South Amboy, and he thought it wouldn't hurt to reach out to the man who hired them.

"Are you sure the paparazzi won't find us?"

"We'll deal with it if we have to, and if Gary is around, we will pick him up on the way. He's waiting to hear from me about Saturday anyway."

"Do you want to call him? You know where the phone is."

Andrew, Robin, and Gary arrived at the Backwaters Grille & Tiki Bar at just after six o'clock that evening. "I wonder if the owner here has seen Alan or Billy," Andrew said.

As the hostess seated them, Andrew asked if the owner was available. "I'd like to say hello."

About ten minutes later, the naturally buoyant Lonnie Carter walked through the restaurant, smiling at the customers and exchanging a few words with a staff member. As he approached Leahy's table, however, the man's demeanor hardened, and his voice was between a growl and a whisper. "Do you know the stress you caused me?"

Andrew was conciliatory. "If you're talking about the eighteenth, I know maybe a week's notice wasn't enough, but..."

"A week's notice would have been manageable," Lonnie said, "but don't stick me with a full house and no entertainment."

Andrew glanced at Gary. "You told him, didn't you?"

Gary rose to his feet. "Alan offered to take care of that. Didn't anyone else from the band contact you, Mr. Carter?"

"No one," Lonnie complained. "No one contacted me. I had a packed house, and everyone wanted to see the Overseas Highwaymen. It's not a marvelous feeling when you get booed. That's for sure."

"Well, we owe you an apology," Andrew said, "but I'd like to explain. Robin and I had to go up north because a friend of mine was in critical condition. My friend was so critical they did not expect her to live."

"I'm sorry to hear that." Lonnie's voice was now gentler.

"There's more!" Andrew continued by describing how Clare had grown up in foster care and never knew her biological mother. "My mission was to find her actual mother before it was too late."

"I admire you for that."

"Since I was away, I asked Gary to tell you, and he transferred that responsibility to another band member. Before pointing a finger at Alan, I'd like to talk to him, but that's what happened."

Gary placed his hand on his chest. "It's my fault, Andrew. I should have called Mr. Carter."

"How is your friend now?" Lonnie asked.

"Robin and I found her mother, and it looks like my friend will be all right."

Lonnie's eyes widened. "That's amazing!"

"I wish I could make it up to you."

"You can. Sign up for the open mic. I'm sure everyone here will enjoy hearing three songs from you."

"Sure, but I didn't bring a guitar with me. I only came in for dinner."

Lonnie grinned. "I'll arrange for you to have a guitar. Just put your name on the sign-up sheet."

Gary glanced at the stage area. "Is a spare bass in the house?"

Lonnie waved over a young man with a tray of water glasses. "Joey, bring their bill to me at the end of the night."

"Oh, Lonnie," Andrew protested, "that is not necessary."

"It's my pleasure. Enjoy your dinner."

After Joey took their orders, Robin giggled. "Oh wow, Andrew! That was smooth."

"Lonnie is a good guy. He knows I'm not jerking him around."

After sipping his water, Gary said, "Here's my suggestion. Even if we're not playing Saturday, let's show up and support the camp."

Andrew gave a thumbs-up. "Good idea! Alan and Billy will be there. It could be very interesting."

28

CAMP TURTLE COVE

SATURDAY, JUNE 1, 1985

O n Saturday morning, Andrew and Gary entered the office at Camp Turtle Cove, where Hannah greeted them from behind a counter. "Nice to see you again," she said. "I'm sorry you won't be playing this year."

"That's what we hear," Andrew said. "We stopped by to donate."

"Thank you," Hannah said. "That's very generous of you."

At that moment, Alan Browne, Billy Morris, and a third unknown fellow entered the office. The third fellow was dressed in a collarless linen shirt with a floral pattern, white shorts, and tennis sneakers. Andrew guessed he wasn't part of Alan's new band.

"Good morning, everyone. Name's Rowdy Spike. Is this where Alan Browne's Overseas Highwaymen should check in?"

Hannah showed him the logbook on the counter. "Just one person needs to sign."

Rowdy tapped Billy on the arm. "Morris, take care of it."

Next, Rowdy turned his attention to Andrew. "What about you? Are you a musician? Are you looking for an agent? I'd have to see you play before I'd consider taking you on."

Alan tapped Rowdy on the shoulder. "Rowdy!"

"Not now, Alan," Rowdy said.

"We're both musicians," Andrew said, "but we're not looking for an agent, Mr. Spike."

Billy turned around after signing the book. "Rowdy, you're talking to—"

"That's right, Billy. I'm talking."

Alan and Billy stepped out of the office. "We'll just go check the sound system," Alan said.

"Is this too awkward for you?" Andrew called to his two former bandmates as they headed through the door.

Andrew turned back to Rowdy. "What kind of music do your clients play?"

"Up till now, they've been playing tropical rock, but the band's going to expand their performances with more theatrical stuff—costume changes, props, and so on."

"I mean, what songs do they play?"

"Oh, they've got an album of all originals songs," Rowdy boasted. "You've heard of 'Margaritas at Sunset,' haven't you? That one is always on the air."

"Yeah, we know it," Gary chimed in, "but we thought that was by the Overseas Highwaymen."

Rowdy snickered. "Same band! We're just upgrading the personnel and changing the name to reflect Alan Browne as the band's new front man."

"Excuse me, Mr. Spike," Andrew said. "I have to find Alan and Billy."

"If you're looking for autographs, stick around after the show."

"It's not about autographs."

"I'm the band's business manager," Rowdy Spike said. "Anything you say goes through me."

"Very well, Mr. Spike," Andrew said. "You know who I am. I own the rights to the band's music. Alan Browne and Billy Morris signed contracts when they joined the Overseas Highwaymen so they couldn't do anything like this. Have they told you that?"

"No, Mr. Leahy. I admit I haven't heard this before, but we can challenge those contracts in court. Of course, I'd like to consult with our legal team."

Andrew was sitting in the catbird seat. "If you send your clients onstage today, you'll be risking serious legal entanglements."

"You can't stop us today, Leahy! We're already booked."

"Think about it! You haven't read the guys' contracts. Your counsel hasn't read them, so you don't understand the legal ramifications. This isn't even a paid gig. It's a fundraiser. You have nothing to gain and everything to lose."

"I see what you're saying, Leahy," Rowdy admitted. "I'll get back to you."

"No need to get back to me. We'll be watching."

After Rowdy Spike left the camp office, Gary slapped Andrew on the shoulder. "Man, you sent the dude out of here with his tail between his legs. Well played."

Later in the day, as Andrew and Gary watched campers work on their kayaking skills, Charles Harris approached from across the beach. "Can I talk to you?"

Andrew and Gary exchanged quizzical glances.

"Let me cut to the chase," Mr. Harris said. "Alan Browne's Overseas Highwaymen dropped out of today's program, and I wonder if you would play a set."

Andrew checked his watch and agreed. "It looks like we have time to retrieve our instruments. Yes, we'd be happy to play."

"Mr. Harris," Gary asked, "what happened to the other band?"

"I don't know. According to Mr. Spike, something came up, whatever that means."

29

CLARE'S CALL

By late June, the Overseas Highwaymen dropped out of the national limelight. There would be no Northeast tour for Andrew and Gary, so they passed the summer of 1985 by writing and rehearsing new music. After Labor Day, they planned to rejoin the South Florida music scene.

One evening, while working out some lyrics, the wall telephone rang. Andrew wasn't expecting to hear from anyone. He thought it might be Robin, but it wasn't.

"Andrew? It's Clare!"

Andrew fired a barrage of questions. "I'm so happy to hear from you! How are you? Where are you? How are you feeling?"

"First, I'm staying with my mother and her husband in Spring Lake. I want you to know how much I appreciate that you found Doreen and brought us together. How did you ever do that?"

Andrew didn't know how much Clare remembered about her out-of-body experience or whether he should even bring it up. He deferred that question for the moment. "I had help, but we can talk about that later. For now, I want to hear how you are doing."

"Well, I'm regaining my strength, doing physical therapy. My doctor expects a full recovery, which is nothing short of remarkable. Soon I'll be back to work."

"I guess you mean the restaurant."

"Oh, you know about the restaurant? I guess Mom told you I'm partners there with my boyfriend, Sam."

"I met Sam when we all convened with your neurologist. Sam, Jason, Doreen, and my friend Robin and I were there."

Clare chuckled. "I know. Mom told me you pretended to be my brother so you could see me. That was sweet. I'm glad you didn't get caught."

"That would have been embarrassing. I don't regret it, though."

"I want to hear about the Overseas Highwaymen and how you became a rock star. Aren't you're coming to the Northeast for some shows?"

"The band won't be touring. We're no longer together." Andrew updated Clare on what had happened among the band members. "Alan and Billy moved to Nashville, but I still have my buddy, Gary, on bass. We'll be playing gigs here by early September."

"Oh, I'm sorry to hear that. Mom and I were hoping to see you in New York. I'm sure I'll be well enough by then. Do you plan on returning this way?"

"Not right now," Andrew said, although he would have dropped everything in a heartbeat and rushed off to see Clare if the relationship didn't feel like it did in college—in the *friend zone*. Back then, Jason had stood in the way. Now it was Sam.

"Clare, tell me about your coma. I mean, do you have any recollection?"

"Yes, I had this coma-dream, but the details are sketchy. I keep the details in a notebook to help me remember. The doctor thinks these are false memories, fabricated by my brain since coming out of the coma. The doctor says my brain was too sick to even generate dreams. I guess it must sound crazy when I tell him about it."

"I'd like to hear the specific details—anything you remember."

"Hold on a minute," Clare said. "Let me refer to my journal." After a moment, she described being in a spiritual realm, where she met a spirit guide whose name she couldn't recall. She described a beautiful wooded area with a lake, where she met important people, but couldn't remember who they were either. "I wish it wasn't so fragmented. In the dream, I kept wondering whether I would live or die."

"That's very interesting." Andrew wondered if Clare would think his next question was odd. "Do you remember if I was in this dream?"

"I don't think so."

"Was Sam in the dream?"

"That's the thing, Andrew," she said. "I think Sam was in the dream, but I can't remember. In two days, I will meet with a neuropsychologist. His specialty is unlocking the unconscious mind, and he has a new office on Bay Street in South Amboy."

Andrew wanted to remind Clare how she had witnessed Sam's liaison with a teenage girl. Instead, he thought she should recover that memory on her own. "Let me know how it goes with this neuropsychologist."

"Will do," Clare said. "I hope I learn something."

30

DR. EMIL

C lare had driven nothing like Dr. Allen's brand-new 1985 Ferrari 288 GTO. The red two-door sports car sped up from zero to sixty miles per hour in five seconds as she pulled onto the northbound highway to meet the renowned neuropsychologist. Upon arrival, she drove to the end of Bay Street, where a simple white cottage came into view. She parked and approached on foot, noticing the way the property had a nourishing influence on her spirit.

There was a young girl standing on the porch. "Excuse me," Clare said to her. "I wonder if I'm in the right place."

The girl grinned. "Yes, Clare! You're in the right place."

"How do you know my name?"

"You're our only appointment today. You must be Clare."

Something about this girl was familiar. "Have we met before?"

The girl giggled and covered her mouth with her hand. "On nice days, Dr. Emil has sessions on the porch or around the grounds."

"Are you the doctor's receptionist?" Clare asked, thinking the girl looked too young for the job.

"I suppose I am." The girl laughed more quietly this time.

A second later, the front door opened, and a tall man with a long, cozy, tactile beard stepped out carrying a bag of birdseed. "Would anyone like to feed the birds?"

"Are you Dr. Emil?" Clare asked.

"The answer is yes if you're here to explore your unconscious mind. I'm Dr. Emil."

Clare blurted out the purpose of the appointment. "Yes, that's why I'm here. I was in this coma and had this crazy dream. I want to recover the details of the dream."

Dr. Emil held up the bag of birdseed. "Take a handful and throw it onto the grass."

Clare protested. "Shouldn't we get on with my appointment?"

Dr. Emil expressed a warm tone. "Birdseed is part of the therapy. You may think it is unconventional, but *birdseed therapy* has great efficacy. Well-reviewed by the Highest Authority. Hold out your hand."

Clare took some of the seed and threw it onto the grass. At once, several birds arrived out of nowhere. When she threw out more seed, additional birds appeared. Sparrows, goldfinches, blue jays, and black crows were all attracted by the offering. A robin settled on the grassy ground but showed no interest in the seed. Instead, the bird hopped closer toward Clare.

Clare leaned down and addressed the robin. "The seed is for you."

"That bird, a sort of liaison between worlds," the receptionist said.

Clare had heard the phrase—*liaison between worlds*—before, but she couldn't remember where. "Excuse me, but what do you mean by that?"

The girl's answer was cryptic. "Oh, you'll figure that out."

"The next part of your treatment will be in the backyard. Cassandra will show you the way," Dr. Emil said.

"Cassandra?" Clare asked. "Your name is Cassandra?"

"Yes, but call me Cassie."

"Excuse me for asking," Clare said, "but is Jerome your first name? Is Emil a shortened version of Emiliani?"

Dr. Emil smiled. "Clare, you are making excellent progress! Please follow us around back now. There's another member of our staff I would like you to meet."

Cassie led the way to a large, wide-open field at the rear of the cottage. When Cassie whistled, a chestnut-colored horse appeared in the distance and galloped right up to her. She whispered something in the horse's ear, but Clare couldn't hear what she said.

"As you may have noticed," Dr. Emil said, "Cassie has a way with animals. It's almost as if she speaks their language."

"A horse whisperer?" Clare chuckled.

Cassie furrowed her brows. "It's not as though I speak Prince's special equine language. This horse is strong of will, but I don't seek to break him. Rather than using whips and fear the way traditional trainers do, I whisper to him. I approach all animals with love and kindness."

Dr. Emil offered the stallion a carrot. "Prince does not live in a corral. He runs free. If we need him, Cassie can always find him."

Clare remembered the carriage ride with Andrew. "Prince was the name of the horse in my dream. He pulled the carriage when Andrew took me for a ride around the lake in Autumn Haze Park."

"Good, Clare!" Dr. Emil exclaimed. "What else do you remember?"

"I remember Andrew saying he loves me." Even as the words escaped her lips, she felt amazed at how the memory popped into her mind.

"How does that make you feel?"

"It was sweet. I believe Andrew thinks he loves me, but love is only an illusion. Some people have strong infatuations, but love has no permanence."

Tears trickled down Cassie's cheeks. "She doesn't get it."

Dr. Emil concurred. "I've seen this before. They seek love. Yet, when love is in front of them, they can't recognize it or become paralyzed by fear."

Clare considered the extent to which she'd lived a life based on fear and mistrust. She grew up believing her mother didn't want her; she placed her hopes and dreams in Jason only to have him cheat on her. If Sam ever had to choose between her and alcohol, Clare was certain he wouldn't choose her. *No wonder I have trust issues*, she thought.

As if reading her mind, Dr. Emil continued, "Doreen didn't reject you. She did what she thought was right. Now she's trying to make up for it by taking you into her home and helping you get back on your feet. Continue to share your stories about growing up in foster care with her. Painful though it may be for both of you, it is a necessary detox experience."

"What about Jason?"

It was Cassie's turn. "You can't change what happened with Jason and Janine, but you can change how you see the situation. Your task is to let go of whatever judgment you harbor from your husband and former colleague. Do that and ease your pain."

"And Sam?"

"Again, you can change your perception of your relationship with him," Cassie said, "but you can't change Sam. Think of him as part of the Universe's design for your growth and enlightenment."

"So, do you mean I should take care of myself even as I support Sam in his recovery from alcoholism?"

"Sam hasn't hit bottom yet, but that's not what I mean," Dr. Emil said. "Sometimes the purpose of a relationship is to expose a person's wounds. Consider the extent to which fear and mistrust have blocked your relationships."

It was a valid insight. Clare had grown up believing her mother had abandoned her, and her relationships with men were based on the fear of being alone. "Maybe you're right," she said.

Dr. Emil checked the backyard sundial. "Our session is about to expire. You've made some good progress today, Clare. The rest is up to you."

"Wait!" Clare said. "Should I make another appointment?"

An instant later, Dr. Emil, Cassie, Prince, and the entire Bay Street Extension disappeared, leaving behind only the wind blowing the American beach grass back and forth like hundreds of small green flags.

Bewildered, Clare sauntered toward the car and remembered more from the coma. She recalled observing her body at the hospital, meeting Cassandra and Paul, and that Andrew was the only one who could see her. *It wasn't a dream!*

Assuming Sam would be at the café, she drove across town to the house she shared with him. She thought she'd pick up a few items of clothing to bring back to Spring Lake. As she approached the house, however, she noticed Sam's car in the driveway. After parking on the street, Clare entered using the house key hidden under the welcome mat.

From the foyer, Clare could hear the television in the family room. She called out, "Sam? Are you here? It's me, Clare!"

She found him sound asleep on the couch, snoring up a storm with one empty vodka bottle and another half-empty bottle of something else on one of the end tables. "Sam, wake up! Shouldn't you be at work by now?"

Sam didn't stir until Clare laid the car keys on the table and clicked off the TV. "Who are you?" he asked, rubbing his eyes. "Clare? Oh, I thought you were still at your mother's."

"I came up here for a doctor's appointment."

"How did that go?"

"Helpful."

Sam grumbled. "Make a pot of coffee and grab the aspirins? Everything's in the same place. Nothing's changed."

"I can see that."

Sam let out a burst of anger. "Coffee and aspirins—*now!*"

"You know where they are," Clare said with defiance in her voice.

Sam stood up and squinted at Clare. Instead of raising a hand to her, he stumbled to the window and moved the curtain. "Look at that car out front! I wonder who it belongs to."

"That's Dr. Allen's car. He let me borrow it for my appointment since I didn't have my car in Spring Lake."

"I'm impressed," Sam said. "Do you think he'd mind if I took it for a spin?"

"No, Sam! You can't drive the Ferrari. You're too stinking drunk, and I promised no one else would go near it. Dr. Allen needs it back by this afternoon, so I'd better be going."

Sam smirked. Taking a few steps toward the table where Clare had placed the car keys, he snatched them in his hand. "These must be the keys, huh? I'm sure the owner won't mind if I take a little bop around town."

Clare grabbed for the keys, but Sam pushed her away. She pleaded with him. "Sam, don't do this. Why don't you let me drive? One time around the block. Give me the keys."

Sam wore only boxer shorts, a long-sleeve dress shirt, and navy-blue socks as he went out the door to the sports car.

Clare screamed at him. "Sam, you're in your underwear!"

"So are you—underneath."

"You're so hilarious!"

Sam gunned the engine, and the Ferrari disappeared around the corner, a disaster in the making.

31

THE MANGROVE

Three weeks later, Andrew and Gary played a last-minute gig at the Mangrove on Sugarloaf Key. This was their first gig since parting ways with Alan and Billy. "It's a full house," Gary said, unpacking his bass with the glossy black finish. "We're still relevant."

Playing on a small wooden stage, Andrew and Gary opened the show with "Margaritas at Sunset," Leahy's most recognizable song, and the crowd expressed its appreciation with a generous round of applause.

Just as the ovation was dying out, Andrew saw her—Clare—zig-zagging around the honey-hued wooden tables and making a bee-line toward the stage. Andrew couldn't believe his eyes. Although he had told Clare about this scheduled performance, he never expected her to show up.

The fellow in charge of security intercepted Clare and prevented her from getting through.

"It's all right," Andrew said over the microphone. "Let her go. She's with me." *She's with me*, Andrew thought. *If only it were true*.

Clare pushed her way to the stage. "Andrew, when you get a break, we have to talk. There's so much I have to tell you about my coma-dream."

143

Although this was an ill-timed moment, Andrew embraced Clare in front of the audience. He shouted back to Gary, "Take over. Use my six-string. I'll be right back."

"What should I do?" Gary asked.

Andrew held tight to Clare's hand. "Try out some of your songs and see how the audience likes them."

Andrew escorted Clare to the last row of parking, where the only illumination came from a floodlight mounted on a pole. Andrew felt like he and Clare were teenagers again, sneaking away from prying eyes.

"Clare, what are you doing here?"

She feigned a scowl. "You should be happier to see me."

"I'm happy to see you," Andrew assured her. "It's just that you catch me by surprise every time you materialize."

Clare chuckled. "This time I didn't *materialize*. I arrived on a commuter flight from Miami."

"Are you okay? Your health, I mean, how's your health?"

"I still get tired, but I'm okay. What's important is I remember what happened to me while in a coma."

"You do?"

"I had that appointment with the neuropsychologist. I told you about him on the phone."

"Yes, you described him as an expert at retrieving lost memories."

Clare rolled her eyes. "Dr. Emil's expertise is more than that."

"I don't understand."

"Anybody else would think this is insane, but I think you'll understand. As you know, while I was in a coma, my spirit was out of my body, and I had this spirit guide who called himself Jerome Emiliani. He would appear as a medical doctor or as a neuropsychologist. But what I don't understand is why only you could see me in my spirit form."

"Any answer I give you is speculation. Maybe you needed me, a physical person, to find your mother in the physical world."

"Listen, that could be part of it, but I want you to know I remember our carriage ride around the lake with Prince."

"Oh?"

Clare smiled. "Yes, and I remember what you said just before you vanished."

"Wow! I thought that was just a dream. I'd fallen asleep on Uncle Ed's couch. When I woke up, I figured the carriage ride was a vivid dream. But you remember it too?" He stopped talking for a moment, thinking he'd heard someone walking nearby.

"Is it true what you said before you disappeared?" Clare asked.

"It's as true as can be. Since graduation, I've wanted one more chance to tell you, though I never thought it would be under such unusual circumstances."

Clare's eyes welled with tears. "Tell me again."

In that tender moment, a sudden barrage of flashbulbs lit up their secret hideaway. Two men emerged from behind a parked car carrying cameras. "Excuse me, Andrew," one said. "May we get a word with you? Who's your new girlfriend? What happened to Lady Nadia?"

Damn paparazzi, Andrew thought. *I wish they'd forgotten about me.*

Disregarding the reporters, Andrew led Clare back to the stage area. "We can talk more after the show," he said, stepping back onto the stage with Gary. "Do you have a place to stay?"

"I'm staying at the Barbary Manor, a bed-and-breakfast off Duval Street."

"I know where it is. Robin lives across the street, and I'm acquainted with Mrs. Gardner, the manager," he shouted back, not sure if she'd heard him.

Clare stayed for the entire show and waited while Andrew signed some autographs and spoke to anyone who wanted to say hello or ask a question.

"You are very popular, aren't you?"

Andrew shrugged. "Can I give you a ride back to your place in Key West?"

Clare declined. "No, I rented a car at the airport. It's so late now. I think I'm ready to call it a night."

"How long will you be around?"

"Just for the weekend," she said. "I have to get back and oversee the restaurant. Sam's in jail, you know."

"Jail?"

"Sam smashed up Dr. Allen's Ferrari—totaled it. Sam was driving drunk on the revoked list, smacked into a police car, and left the scene of the accident. I was the one who called the police because he would have hurt himself or someone else. His lawyer says he'll do time. We just don't know how much time he's facing."

"Anyone hurt?"

"A police officer had a bump on the head that required stitches. Sam was so drunk he doesn't even remember taking the car."

"I imagine Dr. Allen isn't thrilled."

"He's furious! Can you blame him?" Clare shook her head in disgust. "It gets worse, but I don't want to talk about the other problem."

"Do you mean Lydia?"

"You know about that?"

"You told me when you were in spirit."

"That's right, I did," Clare remembered, "and that will complicate my boyfriend's legal difficulties."

Andrew concluded Clare and Sam were still committed to one another, no matter how angry she may have been with him. After all, hadn't she just referred to Sam as her *boyfriend*? And wasn't she overseeing the restaurant for Sam?

By the time Andrew walked Clare to her rental car, the parking lot was empty. "Do you have plans for tomorrow? Can I show you around Key West?"

"I have a flight back late tomorrow afternoon," Clare said. "Can we get together in the morning, say, around ten o'clock? It doesn't matter what we do."

Andrew's casual goodnight kiss on Clare's cheek expressed friendship, but his eyes sent a message that said much more.

32

CHANGE OF SCHEDULE

C lare awoke the next morning in her room at the Barbary Manor, realizing the same unique energy still existed between her and Andrew. During four years of college, Clare had in Andrew a friend who helped her study for exams; he was also available to listen to her fears and needs. Warmed by this thought, she went downstairs for breakfast on the wraparound porch. Mrs. Gardner, a woman of about fifty with silver hair, seated her with a young married couple from England, by the names of Clive and Elizabeth.

Elizabeth rambled on about their plans for the next two weeks in Key West. Hearing the couple's itinerary made Clare wish she could have arranged for a longer stay, but as she explained to her tablemates, she had a restaurant to run. "I'm just here for the weekend."

Clive dabbed a napkin on the corner of his mouth before taking a sip of tea. "Pity," he said, referring to Clare's time constraints. "Later, we'll meet with the psychic across the street. It's Elizabeth's idea. I think it's a bunch of rubbish."

"Stop it, Clive! Lady Nadia is Key West's 'most gifted psychic.'"

"I understand Lady Nadia is very good at what she does," Clare said, regarding the narrow, rectangular shotgun house.

"Have you met Lady Nadia?" Elizabeth asked.

"Not formally," Clare said, "but she's a friend of a friend."

This time, Clive's sarcasm came across with more force. "Lizzy, we can't get a better recommendation."

"Clive, you're being rude to our tablemate, and I hate it when you call me Lizzy."

Clare tried to defuse the moment. "So, when did you two get married?"

"Today is our first wedding anniversary," Elizabeth said.

"Congratulations!"

"Yes!" Clive chuckled. "Lizzy wants to know if Lady Nadia can tell us if we'll have financial success."

"Lady Nadia is a relationship psychic. She may not answer that question," Clare said, "but enjoy your reading."

After Clive and Elizabeth finished their breakfast, Clare sat alone, nibbling on her last piece of toast, when Mrs. Gardner approached the table. "There's someone named Sam on the phone for you. I offered to take a message, but he insists it's an emergency and needs to speak to you right away."

"Sam, did you say?"

"Yes, follow me to my office. You can take the call there. Push the button to pick up the line."

Reluctant to talk to Sam, Clare followed Mrs. Gardner. She exhaled before pushing the blinking button. "Hello."

"How could you leave me in jail?" Sam demanded.

Clare maintained her composure. "Sam, it's so good to hear your voice. I'll be home tomorrow. Don't pick me up at the airport. I have a ride."

Anger burst out of Sam like an F5 tornado as he went into an incomprehensible rant. In the end, he demanded that Clare return home. "Change your flight if you have to," he said. "Just get here or else." He slammed the telephone.

Still seated at the manager's desk, Clare noticed her trembling hands, unnerved by Sam's last words—*or else*. He sounded more threatening than ever.

Mrs. Gardner poked her head in the door. "Is everything okay?"

"Yes, everything is fine, but I'm going to check out early. May I call my friend Andrew to tell him not to pick me up? I have to catch him before he leaves his house. It's a local call."

"Go right ahead, dear."

Clare called Andrew, but there was no answer. Frustrated, she checked out of the Barbary Manor, returned her rental car, and switched to an earlier flight home. She also left a written message for Andrew with the manager.

Knowing that parking could be a challenge in Key West, even on side streets, Andrew had the privilege of using Robin's private driveway. He noticed a certain spring in his step, thinking of spending the day with Clare. As he crossed the street, Andrew spotted staff clearing tables on the front porch.

Mrs. Gardner greeted him at the front step. "I knew someone named Andrew would arrive any minute, but I didn't know I would get a visit from *the* Andrew Leahy."

"How are you, Mrs. Gardner?"

"Nice to see you again," she said. "You must be here for Clare."

"That's right."

"I'm sorry, but she checked out not more than a few minutes ago."

"Checked out?"

Mrs. Gardner nodded. "She received an urgent call. I let her use the phone in my office. She left for the airport right after the call."

Andrew wondered if there was a problem at the restaurant. "I don't mean to be nosy, but any idea who called her?"

"The caller identified himself as Sam."

"Sam?"

"That's right, but Clare left a note for you. If you'll wait here, I'll get it from my office."

"Thank you."

Mrs. Gardner returned with an envelope addressed to him, and Andrew stepped aside to open it.

Andrew,

Please accept my apology for leaving. Sam is out of jail, and he's tracked me down. I don't know how he found me here, but he did. I've got to go home. Sorry we couldn't spend today together as planned, but I'll call you soon.

Clare

Andrew walked across the street to Robin's house. By the time he reached her sidewalk, Robin opened her front door. "Hey, what's going on?" she asked. "I saw you talking to Mrs. Gardner."

Andrew updated Robin on how Clare had surprised him at his show and that they had planned to spend time together.

"Sam had been in jail on several serious charges, but now he's out. He found Clare at the Barbary Manor and persuaded her to return home."

"She must have gone to the airport. Why don't you look for her?"

"Although she now understands my feelings, Clare's commitment is to Sam.

"I don't know what else I can say to her."

"It's not time to give up."

Andrew averted Robin's gaze. "Oh, I've been hoping Clare and I would end up together, but that's not a prayer worth throwing into the cosmos."

Robin ushered Andrew to her front door. "You're wrong! The Universe is giving you one last chance. Go after her, Andrew! Go after her!"

33

TRAPPED

SUNDAY, JULY 21, 1985

U nnerved by Sam's call, Clare changed her flight schedule without thinking it through well enough. She switched to a flight with a long stopover in Charlotte, and the net result was such that she advanced her arrival time by only one hour from her original schedule.

Since it wasn't yet closing time, Clare had the Yellow Cab driver take her from the airport to South Amboy Marina Café. There was a sign on the front door: Closed until further notice. Clare paid the driver and stepped out of the cab and into a briny breeze blowing in from Ampoge Bay. Overhead, graphite clouds obscured the light of the moon.

Entering the semi-dark restaurant, Clare detected the smell of gasoline. "Sam, are you here?"

The lights switched on, and she saw Sam standing behind the counter holding a half-empty bottle of vodka. There was another empty bottle near the coffee maker.

"Sam, why were you in the dark?"

"Never mind," Sam said, slurring his words. "Go to the kitchen. I'm going to tie you up."

"Sam, you're drunk. Let's go home so you can sleep it off. You're not tying anybody up."

Sam pulled a handgun from beneath the counter and brandished it at Clare. "Get in the kitchen. I'm not telling you twice."

Clare saw no alternative to Sam's demand. She did what he told her.

Staggering, Sam approached her with the gun. "I'll tell you what is going to happen tonight."

"Wait a minute, Sam! I hope you're not thinking of doing anything stupid."

"Stupid!" Sam pushed Clare through the swinging door into the kitchen. "I'll tell what's stupid, calling the police when I was driving without a license. That was stupid." He grabbed some rope from a drawer and motioned for Clare to sit on a straight-back chair. As he was binding her hands, arms, and legs, Sam warned Clare not to scream or call for help. "No one can hear you, but if you get too noisy, I'll have to gag you." He checked the knots. "You're not going anywhere."

Sam opened another bottle of vodka and grabbed a dirty water glass from the sink.

"Shouldn't you at least rinse out the glass?"

"Stop nagging. It doesn't matter. Dirty glass or clean—makes no difference."

"What's that supposed to mean?"

Sam sneered. "This is my last night on earth. I'll die in a blaze of glory, and now you can join me."

Clare realized why she had smelled the gas. "No, Sam! You can't do this. Just untie me. You need help. Let me get you some help."

"Too late," Sam said. "I'm not doing prison time. After soaking the building with gasoline, I can light a match. It's better this way."

He swallowed a long drink of vodka straight. "Death by fire, it's kind of cleansing, don't you think?"

"But I don't have to die!" Clare pleaded.

"Yes, you do. You've been unfaithful to me."

"No, I haven't."

"Don't lie. I know Andrew Leahy is not your brother. He's your lover, and you went to Florida to be with him."

"Andrew is my college friend. We're not lovers. He found my biological mother. And I went to Florida to thank him."

"He's a big star, isn't he?" Sam laughed and took another swig. "Leahy isn't right for you. He sleeps with a different groupie every night. You shouldn't be with a person like that."

"Andrew isn't like that, and I already told you. We're not together."

"Do you know how I found you?" Sam laughed again. "It was child's play. You wrote the name, address, and the number of the Barbary Manor on the notepad. That information was imprinted on the next page. I rubbed a lead pencil across the paper to reveal what you had written."

"Why did you close the restaurant?"

"I told the staff we were going out of business." Sam laughed. "I didn't tell them the business was going up in smoke."

"What's the gun for?"

Sam's answer stunned Clare. "To blow my brains out once the fire gets going. I mean, I want to be dead before my body catches on fire."

"Please, Sam," Clare begged, "I don't want to die."

Sam mimicked Clare in a high-pitched, whiny voice. "I don't want to die. I don't want to die! After sneaking off the way you did, you deserve to die, Clare. And you will die!" This time Sam's laugh sounded so maniacal it sent shivers down Clare's spine. *Ahahahahahaha! Ahahahahaha!*

Sam pulled up a chair about six feet away from Clare and grew quiet. He continued to drink from the vodka bottle without talking. When that bottle was empty, he got another one. After consuming most of that bottle, Sam dozed off.

With her eyes focused on the wall clock, Clare twisted her wrists to loosen the rope, but the knots were just too tight.

34

SHOWDOWN

Back in Key West, Andrew booked a flight arriving in the Northeast by one o'clock in the morning. After his plane landed, Andrew hailed a cab and gave the bearded driver Uncle Ed's North Point Road address in South Amboy. The driver glanced in his review mirror and asked, "Do I have a celebrity in my cab? I think I know you, don't I?"

Andrew nodded. "You might."

The driver slapped the steering wheel. "You're Andrew Leahy. That's who you are! You're that singer from Florida." He leaned over the seat to offer Andrew a handshake. "My name's Emil."

Andrew always remained personable whenever anyone recognized him. "Nice to meet you, Emil," he said, greeting the driver by name. "Have we met before? You seem familiar."

Keeping his eyes on the highway, Emil said, "We met when you took Clare for a horse-drawn carriage ride around the lake. Do you remember?"

It took a moment to process. "Jerome, the mysterious man with a horse named Prince?"

"Jerome Emiliani, at your service."

"I suppose it's no coincidence I'm in your cab."

"That is correct. Tonight, the Universe has a prodigious challenge for you."

"Does it involve Clare?" Andrew asked, believing he already knew the answer.

"Yes, which is why I'm sure you will accept this challenge. Sam has Clare tied up in the kitchen of South Amboy Marina Café. I'm taking you there now. Sam has been drinking vodka for two days straight, and he isn't thinking well. Use his condition to your advantage. Sam intends to burn down the restaurant with Clare in it."

"How do you know all this?"

"That's not important right now, but I assure you, my intel is infallible."

"Shouldn't we call the police?"

Emiliani rubbed his beard. "The police will get here. Right now, it's up to you to diffuse the situation."

"I'll do anything for Clare, but I'm open to suggestions."

"That reminds me," Emiliani said. "The latest intel says Sam has a handgun."

"Do you have any other *intel* I might use?"

"Sam splashed gasoline around the restaurant as an accelerant. If he lights a match, poof, it'll be Dante's Inferno!"

Emiliani directed Andrew to look in the seat pocket in front of him. "There's a Swiss Army knife in there. You'll need it to cut Clare's ropes."

Andrew found the multi-tool pocketknife and slipped it into his jeans. "So, it's Sam's gun versus my Swiss Army knife?"

"Classic underdog—is that what you're thinking? It reminds me of David and Goliath." He handed Andrew an unopened bottle of vodka. "You'll need this too."

"Thanks, but I don't drink."

"Not for you!" Emil said. "Take the vodka. You'll think of some way to use it. That's enough chitchat. Right now, your damsel is in distress. Go on, hurry!"

Andrew exited the cab and closed the rear passenger door. As he did so, the cab disappeared, and Andrew stood alone in the dark, deserted parking lot.

Instead of going through the front door, he checked around the windows and peered into the shadowy dining area. He saw tables and booths but no sign of Sam or Clare. He crouched his way around to the side of a kitchen window, where he saw Clare bound to a farmhouse-type wooden chair.

Staggering through the front door with a gas container, Sam doused the steps and exterior walls with the accelerant, filling the air with the pungent chemical smell of gasoline.

Andrew examined the Swiss Army knife. *Jeez, this knife is small*, he thought. *So, I sneak inside, avoid an armed man, and get Clare out. Oh yeah, and hope the place doesn't go up in flames...piece of cake!*

"I need a drink!" Sam cried out to no one there. "A drink! Somebody get me a drink, please!"

Andrew understood why Emil had given him the liquor bottle. He walked into the open and disguised his voice with a Southern accent. "Did somebody call for vodka?"

Sam squinted. "Who are you?"

"Name's Huck," Andrew answered, acting a little drunk himself, "and I was just fixin' to pour me a strong one. Problem is I didn't bring any glasses."

"If you're looking for a drinking buddy, have a seat." Sam motioned for Andrew to sit on the top step.

Andrew needed an excuse to go inside. "Do you reckon I could get us a couple of glasses?"

"Never mind that. We can drink from the bottle. You go ahead, Huck. You brought the bottle. Take the first swig."

Relieved that Sam didn't recognize him, Andrew put the bottle to his mouth without taking in any of its contents. "Wonderful stuff," he said, passing the bottle to Sam.

After Andrew repeated this process a few more times, Sam pulled out a pack of cigarettes. "Do you smoke, Huck?"

"If that's gasoline I smell, you shouldn't be lighting up."

Sam said nothing and put the cigarettes in his shirt pocket.

Andrew had to find a different way to enter the restaurant. "Hey, is the restroom open? I have to use it."

"Just go right here," Sam suggested. "No one will see you at night."

"Man, you don't want me urinating in your parking lot, do you? Where's the men's room?"

"Guess you're right." Sam snickered. "Go in and turn left. It's at the end of the counter. You'll see it."

Andrew stood up. "Thanks."

Once inside the door, Andrew raced to the kitchen and found Clare. He signaled her to remain silent while he used the Swiss Army knife to cut the ropes. "Is there another way out?"

"Back door," Clare whispered. "Follow me." But when she opened the door, Sam was standing there with a lit cigarette hanging out of the side of his mouth and the gun pointing at them.

"I hope you didn't think I forgot about tonight's little bonfire," Sam said to Clare. "As for your boyfriend here, it looks like he'll be joining us."

"Put down the gun, Sam," Andrew said. "No need for anyone to get hurt."

Sam waved the gun. "Shut up, Huck! Both of you get back in here."

Clare glanced at Andrew. "Huck?"

Andrew shrugged. "That's right—Huck."

Once back in the kitchen, Sam ordered Clare to sit in the same chair, and he tied her to it again while keeping the gun trained on Andrew. "The gun has only two bullets. One is for Clare. One is for me. I can't spare one for you unless I have to."

"What are you going to do with me?" Andrew asked.

"I'm going to lock you in the lost-and-found closet. Once I set this place on fire, you'll die of asphyxiation. Kind of ironic, isn't it—lost and found?"

"What's that supposed to mean?"

Sam sneered. "You'll lose your life in the fire, and when they find your body, you'll be nothing but a smoldering husk."

"Sam, you're not well," Andrew said. "There are people who can help you, professional people. You don't have to do this. No one has to get hurt."

Sam motioned Andrew to the rear of the kitchen and used a key to unlock the lost-and-found closet. "Get in!"

Andrew hesitated, knowing if Sam locked him in, he *would* end up being a smoldering corpse. If he didn't, Sam would shoot him dead.

Sam pulled a cigarette lighter out of his pocket and yelled at Andrew, "Get in, or I'll do it now!" He pushed Andrew until he was inside the doorway of the closet.

Andrew noticed a blue umbrella hanging on a hook. He grabbed it, and in one fluid motion, he whacked Sam's gun hand, and the firearm fell and discharged into the floor. Sam dropped the lighter and ignited the flammable liquid, turning the kitchen into a menacing inferno. Within moments, flames climbed the walls and spread to the ceiling.

In the background, Andrew could hear Clare screaming his name. He had to get to her, but Sam was in his path. Even in his intoxicated state, Sam was a formidable opponent, driving Andrew to the back of the closet. However, when Sam bent down to feel for the gun on the floor, Andrew saw his opening and charged by him. Maneuvering his way through the raging flames and thickening smoke, he reached Clare with no time to spare.

She implored Andrew to hurry. "Untie me and make it fast!" To Andrew's surprise, the bindings fell away at the mere touch of the Swiss Army knife. Together, they raced toward the front door to escape the burning building.

A shot rang in the back.

Clare groaned. "Oh, Andrew, we have to see what happened."

Andrew believed Sam had used the second bullet on himself. "We can't help him now. Let's get out of here."

Clare was insistent. "Maybe Sam needs help."

Andrew relented. "I'll look, but you can't stay here. Get outside."

"I can help! There's a fire extinguisher just inside the kitchen door. Sam showed me how to use it."

Flames sprung up as if demons from hell were trying to block their reentry into the kitchen. Using the extinguisher, Clare subdued enough fire to move forward.

By now, Andrew had inhaled too much carbon monoxide,

causing blurred vision and shortness of breath. He confronted Sam, who was still holding a gun, inside the kitchen. "The gun's empty, Sam. Come with us." Together, Andrew and Clare ushered Sam toward the front door.

On the way out, a firefighter met them near the pastry tray. Instead of wearing protective outerwear, this fellow was in his dress uniform. As Andrew got closer, he read the name tag: *Chief J. Emiliani.*

"Oh my!" the chief exclaimed, "a bit more alacrity, everyone, if you please."

An ambulance waited in the parking lot, staffed by a young female cadet member of the first aid squad. Andrew and Clare helped place Sam on a stretcher and accepted oxygen masks for themselves.

Clare surveyed the area, surprised there was only one first aider on the scene. "Are you alone with the ambulance?" Clare asked.

"Don't worry. Help is on the way."

Clare knew the cadet. "Cassie?"

"So, I see you are still wearing the chain and locket."

Clare fondled the locket with her thumb and index finger. "It still doesn't open."

"Try it again. It will open now."

Clare unfastened the heart-shaped locket hanging from her neck. As Cassie had predicted, the heart opened. "There's a picture inside!" Clare examined the image. "Cassie, is this you?"

"Yes, and please show it to Doreen and Dr. Allen. It will let them know I'm all right. If you haven't figured it out yet, I am their daughter."

Clare processed the implication. "Their daughter? But...but that would mean..."

Cassie flashed a wide smile. "That's right. I'm your sister!"

Andrew turned to Chief Emiliani. "Do you have a brother who drives a cab? The fellow who drove me here from the airport tonight looks just like you."

"Excellent observation," he said with a tip of his firefighter's cap.

By the time fire engines and other emergency vehicles from surrounding communities arrived on the scene, the fire raged out of control. Andrew winced. "Clare, I'm sorry, but it looks like a total loss."

"Excuse me, Clare," Jerome said with a note of optimism, "but what are my chances of enjoying another plate of shrimp scampi?"

Clare lifted her oxygen mask. "That depends on what the insurance policy says about arson by the owner."

"I'm not an insurance expert, but it'll work out the way it's supposed to," Jerome said. "For now, I think I best fetch my umbrella."

"I don't understand," Andrew said. "That umbrella in the closet, was it yours?"

"Yes, I'd forgotten it the evening I had dinner here."

"I'm afraid the fire has already destroyed your umbrella," Andrew said.

"It's going to rain soon. I should look for it anyway," Jerome said.

From about twenty feet away, Sam lifted his head and shouted to Emiliani, "Hey, buddy! Don't get too close. It's hotter than hell in there."

Jerome nodded to Sam. "Yes, I imagine it is."

Clare watched her spirit guide walk into the burning restaurant, unnoticed by the emergency personnel battling the fire. "Who is Jerome?" she asked Cassie, "and how did he become my spirit guide?"

"In Catholicism," Cassie said, "Saint Jerome Emiliani is the patron saint of orphans and abandoned children. Jerome will never admit it, but that's who I think your guide is. Since you grew up in foster care, it makes sense for him to have this assignment."

Cassie whistled for Prince, and the horse and carriage came out of the darkness. With his blue umbrella in hand, Jerome Emiliani boarded the carriage, and they disappeared into the night.

As Emiliani had predicted, the heavens let go a downpour of rain. It was a gift to the South Amboy firefighters battling the inferno. The cloudburst quenched the earth but drenched Andrew and Clare to the skin. They pulled each other closer, creating a cocoon more protective than the best rain gear could ever be.

Andrew shielded Clare from the rush of plump raindrops. "What could I have done differently to be closer to you?"

"We were close," Clare said.

"You know what I mean."

Clare thought for a moment. "Well, you could have tried harder."

"You and Jason were a solid couple. I couldn't have done anything then."

"What about now?"

"My feelings have not changed."

In Andrew's eyes, Clare saw a love that burns for eternity. She shook her wet hair, trying to make herself as attractive as anyone could be after a night of fire, smoke, and rain. "Would you like to kiss me?"

Before Andrew accepted her invitation, he brushed a tiny droplet of rain off her eyelash and touched her seductive lips with his index finger. There's something magical about a kiss in the rain, an expression of love so tender it cannot wait for the storm to pass.

The first kiss was long and lingering. The next was a shorter smooch, followed by a third, deep and passionate. "I've always wanted to kiss you like that," Andrew said.

"Oh? And how was it?"

"Euphoric!"

"Well, I should warn you, Andrew Leahy. You'd be taking on a mess, and I'm not talking about crusty dishes in the sink. I mean emotional dishes. My last two relationships left me with some deep-seated trust issues."

"I'd like to help with that."

"Even though you followed me for thousands of miles, found my long-lost mother, and saved me from a homicidal maniac in a burning building, how can I be sure you're the one?"

Andrew smiled. "I have my flaws too."

"Such as what?"

"I have trouble letting go."

"You won't have to let go." Clare pulled him closer. "But this may take some time. Can you handle that?"

"I've got as much time as the Universe will allow."

"I think we should get out of the rain!" Clare said.

Andrew chuckled. "Where's a cab when you need one?"

A police sergeant moved toward them, wearing a yellow raincoat. "You folks shouldn't be out in this weather. Come with me. You can sit in the back of my police cruiser. We need statements from you."

Clare shot Andrew a demure and inquisitive glance. "How will we ever explain it?"

EPILOGUE

Andrew Leahy gave up his life as a tropical rock musician and moved back to South Amboy, where he purchased South Amboy Marina Café. Andrew and Clare rebuilt the restaurant and added an attached 150-seat multipurpose theater, which Andrew dubbed the Listening Room. The new complex opened on April 12, 1986, under the name Clare's Music Café.

Before the release of this novel, Robin Karoly sent me a letter in the mail. She'd written the note as if she'd been reading my mind. With her permission, I have included that correspondence below:

Dear Mr. Schultz,

Thank you for writing the story proposed by Andrew Leahy. I understand your initial reluctance, but the Universe must have assigned this task to you for a reason.

When two souls enter the hallowed realm of love, both must be lithe of heart, or love will turn away. No doubt Andrew related a story filled with imponderable coincidences, accidents, and chance encounters. Such happenings are not capricious. Nothing is random. The laws of the Universe are dynamic and provide us with the keys to overcoming our mistakes. To tap into that spiritual energy answers the call of every heart with love, peace, security, and all the things we associate with a sense of home.

Congratulations on your first novel!

Warmest regards,
Robin Karoly

CPSIA information can be obtained
at www.ICGtesting.com
Printed in the USA
BVHW050258051022
648687BV00002B/138

9 781977 255907